BOOK
SALE

SARATOGA BACKTALK

BOOKS BY
STEPHEN DOBYNS

SARATOGA
BACKTALK

STEPHEN DOBYNS

W. W. NORTON & COMPANY
NEW YORK LONDON

Copyright © 1994 by Stephen Dobyns

Printed in the United States of America

First Edition

The text of this book is composed in Sabon
with the display set in Spartan Medium.
Composition by PennSet, Inc.
Manufacturing by The Haddon Craftsmen, Inc.
Book design by Michael Chesworth

Library of Congress Cataloging-in-Publication Data

Dobyns, Stephen, 1941–
Saratoga backtalk / Stephen Dobyns.
p.   cm.
1. Bradshaw, Charlie (Fictitious character)—Fiction. 2. Private investigators—
New York (State)—Saratoga Springs—fiction. 3. Saratoga Springs (N.Y.)—Fiction.
I. Title.
PS3554.O2S23   1994
813'.54—dc20   93-48029

ISBN 0-393-03659-6

W. W. Norton & Company, Inc., 500 Fifth Avenue, New York, N.Y. 10110
W. W. Norton & Company Ltd., 10 Coptic Street, London WC1A 1PU

1 2 3 4 5 6 7 8 9 0

For C. K. Williams

The thrust came first, accurate, deft, to the quick, its
    impetus and reasonings never grasped.
Then my pain, my sullen, shocked retort, hashed, but
    with nothing like an equivalent rancor.
Then the subsiding: nothing resolved, only let slide;
    nothing forgiven, only put by.

—from *"The Insult,"* C. K. Williams

SARATOGA BACKTALK

I'm a kind of rat. I take it as a compliment. Generally it means I'm not to be trusted. You know, sneaky, always padding along after the cheese, always looking out for number one. Expediency for me is what Disneyland was for Premier Khrushchev: a must-see kind of place. I'm what you call a high-on-pragmatism, low-on-ethics kind of guy.

But I don't start out to be bad. Somehow it just happens, like an accident, a slip on the peel of the moral banana.

Rats themselves, the animal variety, are virtuous creatures. They look after each other and lead upstanding lives. Can they help it if they have pointy noses and beady eyes? Unlike human beings, rats almost never kill each other. I make this distinction because in what follows there are lots of rats, both the human and animal variety. The animal rats were just rats, even though I jumped two feet when the first one darted across my sneakers. The human rats came in all shapes and sizes, and some were better than others. Compared to those particular rats, maybe I'm not so bad after all. But that's what any human rat would say, right? I mean, aren't we in the business of sticking up for ourselves?

My name is Victor Plotz, and I'm fifty-nine years old, or thereabouts. The age when they say you don't waste a hard-on, trust a fart or bust your noggin on dumb ideas. Anybody who tells you I'm any older than fifty-nine, don't listen to him. I'm an entrepreneur in Saratoga Springs, New York: the kind of guy with a lot of irons in the fire. I got some investments, some rental property, some little jobs I do. A buy-low-sell-high kind of guy. I spend a lot of time on the phone, a lot of time driving around. I shoot the breeze, drink a lot of coffee and keep my ears open. I know a few women who trust me with their investments and I even make some money for them. It's a life-style that suits me. I've done that nine-to-five stuff and I have learned that it goes against my genetic makeup.

When I was a young man I worked at Schultz's Men's Furnishings in the city, that's New York City, and spent my days lying to a bunch of glad-handing businessmen about how well they looked in a particular suit before my life changed and old Schultz decided that drunkenness on the job was no way to sell men's clothing, meaning I got fired. I've done this and I've done that, and my life has proceeded as smoothly as a guy falling down a flight of padded stairs, and this occasion with the rats, which I'm now telling you about, began in Saratoga around noon on a sunny Friday in May: May 14th, it was.

I got a friend, a best buddy who lets me walk all over him, and even though I'm a kind of rat, he forgives me. His name is Charlie Bradshaw and he's a private detective. Now, I've done some of that work, but I don't like it. Most of what you do as a private detective is sit around, like you spend a whole week staring at a doorway waiting for some bozo to stroll through it. That's eighty percent of the job. Then there is a less boring fourteen percent when you're driving all over hell's half acre trying to find out what doorway to stick yourself in front of—that part of the job at least gets you into the fresh air. Then there is a dangerous and anxiety-ridden five

percent when you actually confront the bozo. This can lead
to bruises. I've had that happen, and my entire being rises up
in protest against it. Bruises are an intrinsic insult to human
flesh. Then comes the scant one percent of the private detective's job when you get paid and patted on the back, which
is the part I am best at. There is something about the feel of
a nice fat check being placed in the palm of the hand which
combines the most pleasing aspects of sex and Valium.

It was Charlie Bradshaw who got me out of New York
City nearly twenty years ago and brought me to Saratoga
Springs. There's no way to avoid saying it: he saved my life.
I worked for him for a while. He'd been a Saratoga cop, then
head of security for a stable outside of town, then a private
detective. His mother has got a hotel in Saratoga, the Bentley,
and I worked for her as well. But Charlie is a maintenance-
level kind of guy, meaning he tries to keep his life on a certain
steady course: few peaks, few valleys. He's got a small house
out on Lake Saratoga, a girlfriend that keeps his clock clean
and he's got a stack of books about the Old West. Charlie is
in his mid-fifties and has a swimming regimen. In fact, he's
got a lot of regimens, and if someone came along and offered
to hitch Charlie's wagon to a star, he would say no thank
you. I may be talking through my hat, but sometimes I think
Charlie believes that if he didn't keep his life under tight
control, then he would just go whanging off into partyland.
Dance all day, dance all night. His father was a gambler and
his hero is Jesse James, like he can tell you Jesse's collar size
and how he brushed his teeth. On the wall of his detective
office on Phila Street in downtown Saratoga Springs, Charlie
has hung a big poster of Jesse James just like the post office
has hung a big picture of President Bill Clinton.

I've seen customers come into Charlie's office, sit down
and stare at Jesse's rattlesnake eyes, finding something
vaguely familiar about them. A famous policeman? they won-

der. Perhaps a relative? And when they finally make the con-
nection, they tend to look at Charlie in a new light. Some
even get up and walk out without ever stating their business.
And Charlie doesn't mind this. They walk out, so what?
That's what it means to be a maintenance-level kind of guy.
He pays the rent, pays his mortgage, keeps his clock clean
and breezes through his week as easily as a trout flopping
around in a mountain stream. Me, I'm more ambitious. I like
the peaks and endure the valleys. I worked for Charlie for a
few years, then struck out on my own, except for occasionally
helping him with odd jobs. He's happy driving a little car, I
like driving a big car. Don't think I'm being disrespectful.
Charlie is someone who is who he is no matter what. Like
his personality fits him like a condom. This is nothing I
wouldn't tell him to his face. Even in a raging blizzard, he's
Charlie Bradshaw. Me, apart from being a kind of rat, I don't
know who or what I am from one day to the next.

This particular Friday in May I was sitting in Charlie's
office around twelve-thirty using his phone while he was off
at the YMCA swimming his laps. I had some tenants in a
duplex who'd been breaking up the furniture and hadn't been
paying the rent and I had to explain how their ankles would
get busted if they didn't shape up. I find it hard to be threatening on a cellular phone, so I was using Charlie's square
black old-fashioned one. And of course it was his nickel and
I had other calls to make as well. It was a bright spring day
and the windows were open. A couple of pigeons were making
cooing noises on the window ledge and I could hear the sound
of traffic from Broadway.

Charlie's got a drab sort of office over a used-book store.
Two windows look out on Phila, facing the big red brick
building across the street. A scratched oak desk and gray
metal file cabinet, a safe, some visitor chairs, linoleum on the

floor and this big poster of Jesse James in an ornate antique frame behind glass. Originally, he had the poster tacked to the wall, but I kept fooling with it: drawing on an eye patch or giving Jesse a handlebar mustache. Charlie would get mad and stamp around. That's another problem with Charlie—he's got a sense of humor like a gambler's good luck: it comes and goes. So Charlie went out and bought himself a new poster and bought this big frame from an antique store and he screwed the whole thing to the wall just like in one of those upscale fern bars where they are afraid the yuppies will steal the artwork.

Anyway, I was sitting at the desk making my phone calls when there comes a tap tap at the door. Charlie has a small anteroom separated from his office by an opaque glass wall with a door in the middle. On the top half of the door is a sheet of frosted glass with the word OFFICE printed in big black letters, although seated at his desk you see the letters backward so it looks like ECIFFO. And it was against these letters that I saw the knuckles of a hand go tap tap. Tell you the truth, I'd never heard anyone enter the anteroom—that's how caught up I was in my threatening phone call.

"Come in," I called, then I said my rude goodbyes to my tenant and hung up. My tenant is a biker and he revs his Harley in the living room: he says he's tuning it. Tire slashing is too good for him.

The guy who entered the office was a little guy maybe a few years older than me. He was little without being small, or maybe he was small without being little. In any case, he seemed very sure of himself and he walked up to the desk without even glancing around the office and he kept his back straight. He wore a natty blue suit, a necktie that didn't call attention to itself and his lackluster gray hair was scattered across his balding scalp like fragments of grass on a school playground. His eyes were sharp. He looked like money. He looked like he was used to giving the orders and paying the tab.

"Mr. Bradshaw?" he asked.

"I'm his partner and financial adviser," I said, taking my feet off the desk. "Plotz, Victor Plotz."

"Will Mr. Bradshaw be back soon?"

I don't know what it was about the guy's tone that irritated me. Maybe I felt he was being dismissive. There's no sucker you want to catch as much as the sucker who doesn't want to be caught. "That depends," I said. "Mr. Bradshaw's a busy man and I screen his appointments."

"Isn't this his office?"

"Let's say this is the office you get to before you get to his real office. I don't think you told me your name."

The little guy in the blue suit was looking at the picture of Jesse James. I guess if Charlie had other pictures, like a picture of me for instance, then it wouldn't be so striking. And the frame is big and black with gold filigree. Stuck up there on the wall behind Charlie's desk, Jesse James looks like the founder of the firm. The little guy was looking at Jesse as if he were just about to articulate the words "Isn't that . . ." but he was the kind of guy who believes that Doubt is a kissing cousin to Weakness and he wasn't about to show any weakness. Tough—that was the impression he wanted to make.

"I'm Bernard Logan," he tells me in a way supposed to make me think I'm supposed to recognize his name. He gives me a card that says Battlefield Farms and a P.O. box in Schuylerville, a pokey town on the Hudson about ten miles east of Saratoga. "I want to hire a private detective."

I rubbed my hands together in a soothing manner. "Take a seat, Mr. Logan. Mr. Bradshaw is pretty busy right now, but if I know what's bothering you, then maybe I can twist his arm." This was a downright lie, because Charlie hadn't had a case all month, apart from some insurance stuff. I knew for a fact that he was broke. On the other hand, he's got a little garden around back of his house on the lake and in May he likes to spend the warm days fooling with the lettuces and weeding his snap peas.

Logan put his hand on the back of the visitor's chair but couldn't quite bring himself to take the plunge. "This is a sensitive matter," he said.

I shut my eyes, leaned back in the swivel chair and nodded slowly. What was it about his tone that made my skin itch? It seemed to suggest a group of people from which I was excluded. "I see myself as a sensitive kind of guy," I said. "You own this place, this Battlefield Farms?"

"I'm the major stockholder." Logan sat down. It was as if he had just taken the hook into his mouth, and I waited to give the line a tug. Still, there was no anxiety about him, no nervousness. Most people who turn up in a detective's office show some discomfort. After all, they've got a problem. Logan had gray skin, like wet cardboard, and his face showed all the emotion of a guy buying a pair of shoes. "It's a family-run business," he continued. "My wife, plus a son and stepson from my first marriage. We have a lot of horses, both our own and those we train or breed for others."

"And you're near the battlefield?" This was the place where General Burgoyne lost the Battle of Saratoga for the British and where Benedict Arnold played hero. Now it's a big national park a few miles south of Schuylerville right on the Hudson.

"Our land abuts the park. You must know it."

Sometimes in summer the park is full of all kinds of crazy guys with muskets and old-timey uniforms. They run around trying to stab each other with rusty bayonets and shouting like wild men. I wouldn't go near it for a million bucks. "Like the palm of my hand," I said. "You must feel proud living next to the place where history took such a big step forward. I mean, where would we be without the Battle of Saratoga, right? We'd be Canadians, most likely. Or Brits."

Logan gave me his glassy stare, like history for him was just so many dead calendars. "My wife wants to kill me, Mr. Plotz. That's why I'm here."

Well, there were a lot of humorous things I could have said in response to that remark, but I kept my mouth shut and looked concerned. Personally, I think most spouses want to kill one another. It's what marriage is all about. Death practice—that's marriage, which is why I specialize in girl-friends.

"She's younger than I am by almost thirty years and she's got a lover, my own foreman. I guess you've heard this story before, correct? We've been married eight years."

Instead of looking ashamed or embarrassed, Logan looked angry. His fingers were curled into tight little fists and he glowered as if daring me to disagree. I figured I could also make a few wisecracks about the foreman poking his wife, but I hung on to my sympathy face and pursed my lips. After all, I was trying to do Charlie a favor. "What makes you think that she wants to kill you?"

"I heard her talking to Randall, he's the foreman, Randall Hanks. What do they think, that I can't see what they're doing?" Logan's body grew stiff for a moment as if from an electric charge. "She has an insurance policy on me, a big one, and it's new. She and Randall have been carrying on, I don't know, maybe for a couple of months or longer. I heard her talking to him on the phone. She told him that very soon their problems would be over and they'd have the farm. The only way for that to happen would be if I was dead."

"Did she say how or anything like that?"

"No, just that it would be soon."

"Did you actually hear her use the word 'kill' or 'murder'? You know, a violent-death-type word? Maybe she's just been buying Lotto tickets."

Do you know those stares called glacial stares? Narrowed eyes and a curving trajectory down the nose. Even the chin seems more pointed and chilly. Logan gave me one of those, and I gave him a happy smile to show I was basically okay.

"They want me dead. They want the farm. They want the freedom to continue their sexual romp without my interference."

"Where's your proof?"

"I told you I heard her on the phone . . ."

"Look, Mr. Logan, Charlie Bradshaw's a busy man. That's why he's got me to screen his visitors. If I go to him with a story about an overheard phone call, he'll laugh me all the way down to Brooklyn. You got to have some hard facts."

"The insurance policy . . ."

"Hey, I got a policy on my cat. It wouldn't stand up in a court of law."

Logan snapped his fingers at me. "If I had something that could stand up in court, I'd go to the police. I wouldn't bother with a private detective."

I figured he had me on that one, so I cleared my throat and sucked my teeth. "What happened to your first wife?" I asked.

"She's been dead fifteen years. Cancer."

I nearly said, Just like me, because my wife had died of cancer as well, although that was more like thirty years ago.

"And her son works at the farm?"

"There are two. The son we had together, Carl, who's twenty-three and who graduated from Cornell last year. Then there is the son she had by a previous marriage: Donald Croteau, he's thirty-five."

Mentioning these two guys, it was like Logan was talking about warm weather and cold. I had the feeling that Logan didn't waste a lot of love on his stepson, whereas this Carl fellow was the apple of his eye.

"And they all live with you?"

"It's a big farm. There are several houses. Donald has his own place. So does the foreman, Hanks."

"Anyone else?"

"The trainer, Frankie Faber." Logan kept rubbing his hand across his jaw as if it itched.

"One big happy family," I said, and again Logan gave me one of his arctic expressions. "Why don't you just fire the foreman, this Randall Hanks?"

"I used to like my wife, Mr. Plotz, and I'm not much good as a husband. When they started their affair, I pretty much accepted it. Better that she has her fun at home, right? Or at least on the property. She'd had affairs before, but none of them were serious and I didn't much worry about them. This one has become serious. She took another bedroom in the house. We don't talk. We don't get along. She wants me out of the way and by that I mean dead and she wants it to happen as soon as possible."

"What's the rush?"

"I'm not a weak man, and I have a temper. She can see that relations are getting worse. I'll fire Hanks and get rid of her as well, but if you or Bradshaw can come up with evidence that she's trying to kill me, then that will serve my purpose even better, especially in the divorce courts. For a while, even when she was having these little affairs, we stayed friends. Now we're nothing to each other, just money and mutual bitterness. I want her gone; she wants me dead."

"And what's this treasure's name?"

"Brenda Stanley. She used to ride show horses and she kept her own name."

"No kids?"

"She didn't want any."

"What do you want Charlie to do?"

"I want him to come out to the farm and talk to people, make them worried. If Brenda gets scared, then maybe she and Hanks will do something to show their hand."

"Maybe Charlie could yell at them, right? Maybe he could catch them in the act and smack their pink fannies."

Logan looked at me as if I were a tomato splop on his white bucks. "You like your little joke, don't you, Mr. Plotz."

"It's the bane and treasure of my life. When would you like this terrorist visit?"

"They'll all be around tomorrow morning."

"All?"

"My son, my stepson, everybody except Frankie Faber. He's still down at Belmont and couldn't come up. I want Bradshaw to clear the air. You too, the more the merrier. Then stay on for a few days and keep an eye on things. There's some other stuff I'd like to show Bradshaw—a letter I found, and a rattrap."

"What's so suspicious about a rattrap?"

"This isn't so much a trap as a cage. I just want to show it to him. I think it's important."

"You're asking for a bodyguard, not a detective," I said.

"I want someone who will let my wife understand that I know what's she's planning. I want her to be scared."

"I bet you're a swell guy," I told him. Still, I knew that even mean sons of bitches can pay you a living wage and the money from a mean guy and a nice guy smells just as sweet. "This won't be for free, you know. Charlie will need a retainer."

"How much?"

"A thousand bucks."

Logan blinked twice. "That's a lot."

"The pros cost more. Anyway, you don't want detecting, you want bullying, and that's more expensive."

I should say that Charlie usually asks for a retainer of one hundred and fifty, but he was short on funds and I had decided to do him a favor. Besides, I wanted to learn just how hungry Mr. Logan was.

He drew a tan pigskin wallet from the inside pocket of his brown suit coat. "I'll need a receipt."

"Sure thing, and if you want I'll stand on the desk and sing 'Your Achy Breaky Heart.' " That was a lie, I could only remember half the words. I just wanted to give the needle another turn.

·   ●   ·

But sometimes even one's most charitable actions can land one in the soup, because it was no more than thirty minutes later that Charlie was saying to me in a kind of depressed voice, "Victor, you've got to return the money."

He was standing in front of his desk and his hair was still wet from swimming. Some people have black hair, some people have blond—Charlie's got sparse, like it's a quality more than a color, sparse gray. He was wearing a blue seersucker suit that was a little tight on him and his blue tie looked like it had been yanked into about ten thousand Windsor knots too many.

"To ask for a one-thousand-dollar retainer is highway robbery," said Charlie.

"Nah," I tell him, "we were right here in your office."

"Be serious, Victor."

Charlie knows I like him to call me Vic, but he never does. I think he likes the two-beat sound of Vic-tor, like a one-two punch. Whereas Vic has a light and airy sound. Charlie stood with his arms folded like someone who feels he's got reason and righteousness on his side. He's not a big guy, no more than five-ten or so, a little shorter than I am; and he is thickish without being fat, like he's got the build of a freshly baked meat loaf. But his eyes are what you notice straightaway. They're sharp blue eyes and they remind me of Uncle Sam's on those old-timey enlistment posters: "Uncle Sam Wants You!" They are not critical like Uncle Sam's; they are just very attentive. Nowadays his eyes are partly hidden behind bifocals with thin wire frames. Charlie hates these bifocals and keeps taking them off and putting them back on. They make him look grandfatherly, which leads people to think he's a cream puff. Boy, are they sorry.

"Charlie, I'm always serious about a thousand bucks. This Logan guy's got a big problem. His spouse wants to waste him and he's come to you to save his life. Be kind!"

"But I told you I had jury duty next week. There's no telling how long it will take."

"I forgot about that. Won't they let you off for extenuating circumstances? Explain to them that you've got your period."

Charlie sighed and shook his head. "I'm on the jury panel. They may not even choose me."

"Well, there you are. Tell them you're unqualified."

"I still have to be there."

"One thousand smackers, Charlie, there must be a way. Besides, he's counting on us."

"Tell me more about this Logan."

So I gave him back his desk and took the visitor chair for myself. Even though it was past my lunchtime, I told him about Logan's visit. Charlie already knew of Battlefield Farms. It seemed they always had horses running at the big New York tracks—Belmont, Aqueduct, Saratoga—and some of the smaller ones as well. Even Logan was known to him, although only by name, and he had heard of Logan's stepson, Donald Croteau, also. "He was picked up last fall for speeding," Charlie said. "He's got a Porsche that he takes out around five a.m. and sees how fast it will go."

I tried to tell him about Logan's manner, which was still prickling me. It wasn't that he was condescending or too sure of himself, nor was it that the only emotion he had shown was anger; rather, it felt like he was going through a part—not that he didn't believe it, but that he had already practiced it several times. Me, I'm all spontaneity; Logan was studied.

"But I don't see what he wants me to do," said Charlie.

"He wants you to go out there and throw your weight around, to make the wife nervous. He wants you to find evidence against her that will let him breeze through a divorce court. He says he's got it already, some kind of letter and a rattrap, and all he wants is for you to see it."

Charlie had taken off his glasses and was polishing them on his tie. "A rattrap?"

"He said it was a sort of cage. And he's got more stuff besides. Charlie, jury duty doesn't start till Monday. A fast operator like you can wrap this up over the weekend. He says for us to be there ten-thirty tomorrow morning."

"Why ten-thirty?"

"Because that's when they're done exercising the horses. Don't be so suspicious, Charlie! This'll be a piece of cake."

Charlie riffled through the ten hundred-dollar bills on the top of his desk. "A thousand dollars is a lot of money."

"Nah, that was in the old days, Charlie. These days a thousand smackers is no more'n Japanese lunch money. I bet the Pinkertons get that all the time."

Charlie has a number of sore points against the Pinkertons: one, because they blew the arm off Jesse James's mother and killed his half brother, who was just a little kid, and two, because they once turned him down when he was looking for a job. On this particular occasion Charlie pretended that I hadn't spoken. He has a round face and a stubby nose, not many wrinkles for an oldster. He stared over my head as if he were looking at some fat idea floating in the air over by the door like a cherub.

"I guess it wouldn't hurt to go out there," he said.

I stood up. "Great. I'll pick you up about ten in the Mercedes."

"I thought they had repossessed that." There was a slight slyness to his voice.

"I got it back again. I need it to impress my clients."

"Isn't your granddaughter coming to visit next month? What're you going to do about your clients then?"

I sat down again. Charlie had touched upon a tender issue. "I'm praying that my granddaughter will tumble into a well before her school lets out. That may be my only hope."

"Is she stubborn?"

"A half-pint ayatollah."

"I thought she was Jewish."

"They're the worst kinds of ayatollahs. I've talked to this girl on the phone. She's got a missionary zeal that terrifies me. Charlie, I haven't been to temple since my wife died back in 1962. The kid sent me a yarmulke for my birthday. I gave it to the cat. Even the cat won't wear it."

I got a son, Matthew, who works for a hospital in Chicago, a bright boy who's in charge of his own lab. When he was a kid, I called him Matt. Now he wants Matthew, like it's got more weight. He's got a wife, Bernice, three kids and a nice brick house in Evanston. No dog or cat. Pets are dirty, he tells me. Bernice, on the phone she tells me she keeps a kosher kitchen, and I tell her that's nice. Then I make a crunching noise with my teeth and tell her to guess what I'm eating. Carrots? Celery? Nope, I say, pork rinds. Their youngest kid, this twelve-year-old named Susannah, she's the one who wants to come out and visit sometime in June: a nice Jewish girl with the soul of a Baptist missionary. You say, tell her not to come. I've already done that, I've done it five or six times. She says she's already got her ticket; she says she wants to visit her grampa. Back in the late seventies when I had to get out of the city or die there, I nearly moved to Evanston. Matt and Bernice kept inviting me. They're not bad people, they're just dead below their noses. If you ask me, a little evil would give their lives a real boost. And I nearly went, that's how bad those days were. Believe me, if I'd gone to Evanston, I'd be a corpse by now. Either that or in jail. Sometimes it seems that murder is the only way out of a bad situation. Instead of going to Evanston, I called Charlie, even though I hardly knew him. I wasn't grasping at straws, I was grasping at something much smaller than straws. Charlie said, Come on up to Saratoga and I'll get you a job. See what I mean? He saved my life.

2

I got a girlfriend. Actually I got more than one but this is the main one, at least for now, and she's been my main girlfriend for a couple of years and I've got no plans to tell her to take a hike. Her name is Rosemary. She runs a lunch counter out on Route 29 toward Schuylerville. Rosemary Larkin, and what she can do with a cheeseburger would melt your heart. She's fifty-one. She's big and plump and I call her the Queen of Softness. If you ask me, women only come into their prime after they hit fifty. Before that they've got too much bone and muscle: baby machines too easily distracted by what they have manufactured. They remind me of Japanese car companies: all style and no soul. Before menopause a woman can be a real nuisance, she's packed full of hidden agendas and most of them concern her kids. But after fifty a woman's kids are usually grown up and she can turn herself over to pleasure. And they get soft at that age, almost spongy. It's the time when a woman gives up her figure and takes on a shape. Rosemary Larkin has a wonderful pear shape. No aerobics for her. Who wants a lady with a figure like a letter knife?

Rosemary has got this hot tub in her basement and we sit in it and play Elevator. I put my hands under her breasts—big white stocking-cap breasts with nipples like the eye of the cyclops who Kirk Douglas bumped off in that movie about Ulysses. I put my hands under Rosemary's breasts so I can feel their weight, their very consequence and magnitude, and Rosemary calls out: "Eighth floor!" And slowly I raise her breasts up out of the bubbling water. Then she calls out, "Fourth floor!" And slowly I lower them again. Then Rosemary calls out, "Penthouse!" And we go up all the way to her eyebrows. Then she calls, "Bargain basement!" And we go down, down, down.

You can't play that kind of game with a young woman. Not only don't they have the physique for it, but they are too busy with their lives, their careers, their ambition. A woman like the Queen of Softness isn't wound up tight about getting someplace or not getting someplace important, she already lives someplace. She's arrived. She stands on her life with both feet. She doesn't mind that I am fifty-nine, or thereabouts, and that I've got a Jewish Afro and have a figure that yearns to duplicate the Pillsbury Doughboy. We've gone beyond fashion. Our skin is squishy and yielding with black-and-blue marks and adipose tissue and varicose veins. Not only has it been around the track, it has *been* the track. It's been trampled upon. It's been jumped up and down upon. It's got history. We rub each other down with body oil and we're like two great seals flopping together on her big water bed. With thin girls you got to watch yourself. You can cut yourself on the sharpness of their bones. Get a bruise and bleed internally.

I spent Friday night at Rosemary's place. The wind started blowing hard in the night and the windows banged: one of those warm southern winds that seems to carry all your yesterdays along with it. But I didn't want the past. When a day is over, I say fuck it. I been a widower for more than thirty years and that's a long enough time to forget, even though those old pictures can sometimes slap me across the face when

I'm doing no more than looking out the window and smelling the breeze. I put on my cowboy hat and cowboy chaps and Rosemary and me played Hopalong Cassidy. I can lift parts of her, do you know what I mean? The flabby parts under her arms, her belly, the great cheeks of her buttocks, her thighs like sodden loaves of bread—I just lift them up and hold them for a moment. She's got great weight. What with the lifting and the whiskey and the cowboy hat it was nearly dawn by the time we got to sleep.

I had told her about this Logan character, and when I left in the morning, she said, "You take care of yourself. I wouldn't want my sweetie to get hurt."

"A piece of cake," I told her. "There'll be no bruises on this job."

Isn't it always the case that when you make some fool remark like that, you almost always get your neck broke? It's like an axiom or something. I mean, you should carry around a block of wood just to knock on when you need it.

When I reached Charlie's house on the lake shortly after ten, I was feeling hungover and stretched pretty thin.

Charlie met me at the door. He was wearing a gray corduroy coat and a yellow polyester shirt that looked like it had been made by the same people who make Saran Wrap. His gray knit tie had a run in it. "You look like someone beat you up," he told me, pretending to be concerned but not really concerned. His glasses were shiny and his sparse hair was slicked down like he was all set to do business.

"The Queen of Softness," I told him.

Charlie has a girlfriend by the name of Janey Burris. She's a nurse with three kids, all teenagers by now, I think. She's sexy but she's not my type. She has one of those tidy bodies and I'd be afraid I might cut myself on her hipbones, get my throat slashed by a rib. She's got nice lips but has sharp teeth behind them. Nobody can pucker as prettily as a woman who

has lost her choppers: it's the softest kiss in the world. Janey's
been after Charlie to move in with her, to give up his place
on the lake and move back to Saratoga. But there's no way
he will do that. If Charlie doesn't have his time by himself,
his solitude, he gets so gloomy that almost nothing will cheer
him.

Isn't it the truth that you meet someone and everything
seems fine but then you start stepping on each other's toes?
Like I say, Charlie will be Charlie no matter what. Janey
Burris loves him, I'm sure of that, but she also wants to change
him a little, improve him, like someone who buys a nice suit
of clothes and then proceeds to shorten the sleeves, add a
ribbon here and there. The Queen of Softness hasn't started
any of that correction and restoration business, but if she did,
then it's goodbye to the Elevator, goodbye to Hopalong Cassidy and our long nights of pleasure.

"Give me a cup of coffee," I told Charlie.

"We'll be late."

"I'll drink it in the car."

In his house Charlie has pictures of John Dillinger, Billy
the Kid and Willie Sutton. It's a dusty sort of place, although
it's clean enough: bedroom, kitchen and a big living room
with a stone fireplace. It's more of a lair than a house, if you
know what I mean: Charlie's lair. The sofa and armchairs
are big sprawling things with broken springs. The coffee table
wobbles. The big braided rug has some torn places. There
are trees around the house—really just a cottage—so the
neighbors don't seem too close, and he's got a small dock
poking out into the lake. He also has a small aluminum rowboat and sometimes he takes it out on the water and just
sits—no fishing, just sitting and letting the sun bake his forehead, bake his sparseness. Personally, I'd go wacko in a place
like that. I've got an apartment in town right on Broadway,

where the action is. Sometimes I open the windows just to hear the cars honk.

Charlie handed me a steaming cup of coffee. "We've got to hurry."

"I'll drive like the wind," I told him as I held the screen door so he could lock up.

It was a nice day and I drove out along the small roads toward the battlefield. That's all they have out there, small roads. Me, I'm a pavement kind of guy and too much grass makes me agoraphobic. But the winter had been long and nasty and the warm weather felt like a gift, like I had done something right for a change and this was my reward. My car is a lime-green Mercedes 190. It's not new but neither is it cheap. As a matter of fact, me and the bank still have some disagreement as to who it actually belongs to. The Mercedes takes the hills as easily as a young girl on a swing, no sound except from the tires. Charlie has got a Mazda 323. No power, no fifth gear—and the noise it makes is like the sound of worrying—buzz, buzz, buzz—like anxiety personified. It reminds me of a sewing machine in heat. Sometimes I think I bought my Mercedes just so I could ride with Charlie in comfort.

"So'd you bring your gun?" I asked him. Charlie is always forgetting his gun.

He seemed embarrassed and didn't look at me. "I'm not going to take the case."

"You kiddin?"

"Victor, I've got jury duty. I've got other obligations. Besides, I never even talked to the guy."

"You can talk to him now."

"Why'd he want to give me a thousand dollars?" When Charlie gets exasperated or frustrated, his hair starts standing up. It's like something in his brain excites the hair follicles.

"You got a reputation. You're a problem solver. You're the only detective in Saratoga. Maybe he knows your famous cousins." Charlie has three older cousins who are businessmen in Saratoga—serious Republican types with combination locks on their wallets and double underwear in case they dribble when they take a leak. He tries to be nice to them, but they always treat him as if he's been groping fifteen-year-old baton twirlers or has had sex with a goat. Every time Charlie has a successful case, their ulcers act up. Like they can't stand to think of him doing well. But Charlie lived with them for a while as a kid and it makes him think they are something special. I mean, these are guys who wear rubber bands on their weenies. Like their whole lives are spent dividing everything into right and wrong. The wrong stuff makes a Himalaya; the right stuff makes a gopher hill. And I bet you know what they think of me, don't you.

"I talked to James last night. He said that Logan is highly respected. Active in the Lions Club and generous with his money." Charlie spoke as if he were quoting the *New York Times*.

"So this is why you're returning the thousand bucks?"

"I just don't like the feel of it."

It was about five miles to Battlefield Farms. We drove out Battlefield Road, with fields and small farms on either side. Logan's place was somewhere near Bemis Heights, closer to Stillwater than Schuylerville. You get over toward the Hudson and the hills get bigger and the countryside rolls like a lumpy bed. Off to the east the Green Mountains were looking all hazy and warm. The trees still had adolescent leaves and had a feathery look. Cows were up to their knees in black mud. The Mercedes's windows were open and sometimes I'd get a whiff of pig manure.

Battlefield Farms had a big white gate that stood open, and I drove through it. Charlie stopped talking in order to

look the place over. Sometimes he is like a dog on a scent.
For twenty years he was a Saratoga cop, and although he
hates to hear it, he's still got a lot of cop in him. Back in the
seventies just after I met him in New York City, Charlie threw
over his cop job, divorced his wife and moved out to the lake.
I like to tell him that it was me that made it happen but he
just shakes his head and tells me he got tired living other
people's lives.

Logan's driveway was about half a mile long, and I followed it up a hill with a white wooden fence on either side.
In the fields horses were cropping grass. A couple of young
ones were kicking up their heels and bopping around but all
of it angular and jerky as if something above them was yank-
ing their strings. At the top of the hill was a long ranch house:
white with green shutters and some blossoming cherry trees
out in front. On each of the shutters was a golden L. There
was a garden full of daffodils and maybe some tulips: I'm not
up on my flowers. Dandelions, there were lots of dandelions.
Off to the right I could see shed rows and a barn, then another
ranch house, this one smaller. Back from the road not much
could be seen, but driving up the hill to the house, the place
looked like a small village. There was even a training track
with a single black horse with four white stockings and a girl
groom going round and round. The girl's brown ponytail and
the horse's black tail bounced together in complete unison,
like one of those marriages made in heaven.

"If I was a different sort of person, I'd like to own a
horse," said Charlie.

"It'd look cute in your living room."

"You ever think what you might do in another life?"

"Start after women at a younger age: my teens were
wasted on onanism."

"You're impossible," said Charlie.

"Tell that to Onan."

I parked in the circle in front of the house and we climbed out. As we walked toward the front door, I liked how the wind riffled my hair. My hair stands out from my head about three inches, and riffling is a pleasure. It was a little after ten-thirty: about twenty of. I knocked on the door and put on my little smile. Charlie stood behind me looking back over the fields. I could tell he was having sentimental thoughts about what he might do if he were given another life. Personally, I think one life is just about enough for anybody.

After a minute nobody had opened up, so I knocked hard with the soft part of my fist. Another minute passed and still nobody came along. My cheery mood began to dissipate like mist across the surface of a fishing hole. I raised my fist to knock again.

"Let's walk around back," suggested Charlie.

We headed out along the driveway around the house. A dog was barking from somewhere, then I heard someone shout. There was the feeling that everybody was off having a party without us. We rounded the far corner of the house. Attached to the back was a greenhouse with opaque glass. A parking lot with a bunch of cars was next to it. There was another shed row—white with green trim—a hay barn and something that might have been a bunkhouse. The two shed rows and two barns were set out on a hillside that slowly descended toward the Hudson, which twinkled in the morning sun. The hills on the other side of the river had soft loaf-of-bread shapes. Lots of trees had pink and white blossoms, and there was a big oak between one of the shed rows and the hay barn.

"Something's wrong," said Charlie.

I turned away from the scenery and saw people running, about half a dozen of them dashing toward the horse barn. A horse was whinnying so loud that it was more like a scream, and there were banging noises as if the horse was kicking down its stall. Two men were running back from the barn toward the house, coming right at us. The first one was young, no more than twenty-two or so, a handsome kid with black hair and a red plaid shirt.

"Excuse me," I said, "we have an appointment . . ." He ran by as if he didn't even see me. His face was bone-white scared.

The second man was older, chubbier and puffing. I'd seen him around Saratoga in the bars. He hung out at the Parting Glass, one of those modern Irish places where people spend a lot of time toasting one another with Guinness. "Hey," I called, "what's going on?"

He looked at me, surprised, and tried to catch his breath. He bent over with his hands on his thighs. "It's Mr. Logan. He's dead. He's just been kicked to death by a horse."

• ● •

Well, no one paid much attention to us: their lives were moving too fast. It was like wandering around the stage during somebody else's play. They all had their lines, their roles, and we were invisible. Even the chubby guy who I'd seen before at the Parting Glass, Paul Something, was caught up in his own dramatic story, making big memories for himself, something important to look back on.

"His skull's split open!" he shouted at us.

Charlie began to amble a little faster over toward the barn, and I followed. He was all alert while trying to appear relaxed: hands in his pocket, strolling along. The sun kept reflecting off his glasses. He wore a little yellow-and-tan plaid porkpie hat shoved back on his head. I think he keeps that hat just so he will look inoffensive and harmless.

"What do you think?" I asked him. I kept imagining Logan's face as I had seen it the previous day: narrow, gray and sickly.

Charlie shrugged, a one-shoulder-after-another sort of shrug. "Maybe it's an odd coincidence," he said.

About a dozen people stood around the entrance to the barn, both men and women. From inside I could still hear a frantic whinnying and every now and then a thunk or banging noise or someone shouting, "Watch out!" or "Don't get near him!"

The handsome young guy with the red plaid shirt came running back. He was carrying a blanket. It didn't take much to see that he was crying. As he ran into the barn, he kept brushing the back of his hand across his eyes. I was standing near an old guy wearing jeans and a jean jacket. "Who's that?" I asked him.

The guy looked at me curiously. Maybe he wasn't so old. Maybe he was my age. But I carry it better. He had a long droopy mustache and he was chewing one end of it. "That's Carl Logan, the boss's son," he told me.

"Seems pretty broke up."

"Apart from livestock and flowers, he was the only creature the old man cared about."

"You work for him long?"

"Thirty years. You selling something?"

I gave him a peek at my friendly choppers. "In this world, I'm a buyer, not a seller."

As the old guy turned away, Charlie gave me a poke. "Try to be subtle," he said.

"It's my middle name," I told him.

All of a sudden there was more shouting and the sound of hooves on the wooden floor of the barn. "Here he comes!" someone shouted. "Get out of the way!"

The men and women standing around the entrance scrambled to the sides. Where at one moment I had been part of a crowd, now I was standing by myself. Even Charlie had scurried off. Somehow, before I jump, I've always got to consider what I'm doing, but before I had even the least glimmer of an idea I found myself eyeball to eyeball with a big brown horse with three white stockings. Apart from size and species, the only difference between us was that the horse was moving like a lightning bolt and I was rooted to the spot. Even our terror was similar. The horse whinnied and reared up. I couldn't keep from staring at his eyes, which seemed like they were trying to look in a hundred directions at once.

"Victor!" I heard Charlie shout.

My meeting with the horse lasted about a second. As I tried to jump to the left, the horse brushed past me, giving me a shove so I fell back on my fanny. Did I mention that the ground in front of the barn was a pretty muddy place? I splopped down into the mud as everyone watched the horse disappear into a field.

Charlie reached down to help me to my feet. "You all right?" he asked.

I had mud on the seat of my pants and on the palms of both hands. "At least these aren't my Ralph Lauren slacks."

He pulled me up and gave me his handkerchief. Charlie's the kind of guy who always carries a handkerchief. Usually he's got two: one to lend and one to keep for himself.

About half a dozen people came running out of the barn. A thin Texas kind of guy in a cowboy hat was shouting, "Get that horse! I want him tranked. Saddle up!"

Another man shouted, "I'm getting a rifle." He was red-faced and had a belly.

And a woman in a pretty white dress said, "He's my horse and I don't want him killed."

Then there was a lot of other chatter, but what struck me about the thin guy and the red-faced guy and the woman was that they didn't like each other. All three spoke with a bellyful of contempt and bad temper. There were more hoof-beats from inside the barn and a young man, maybe fifteen or sixteen, came galloping out, some kind of stable hand. He looked scared but determined. He took off after the horse, slapping his own horse on the rump. Several other people had run to get horses as well. Down the hill I could see the big brown horse that had almost kissed me tearing along like a locomotive next to a white fence.

I finished wiping the mud off the seat of my pants. They were tan pants, a sort of coffee-and-cream color, and the mud made a big brown stain. I stepped over to the old fellow in the jean jacket. "Who's the thin guy in the cowboy hat?"

"That's Donald Croteau. He's the boss's other son, his stepson actually."

Croteau was giving orders to people. I couldn't tell if he was angry or just had a passion for efficiency. His hat was a ten-gallon pearl-gray hat with a snakeskin band. He had reddish-bronze skin with freckles: a smooth, unlined face, although he must have been in his mid-thirties. His eyes were a dark blue color that I wouldn't mind having myself: dramatic. He was a tense-looking guy with white teeth and a strong jaw, and he kept slapping the fist of his right hand into the palm of his left. This was the fellow who liked to race a Porsche on the back roads of Saratoga County at five o'clock in the morning. To me he looked like someone who would be no pleasure to work for: a guy who likes to make people jump and then shouts at them for not jumping fast enough.

"And who's the frail in the white dress?" She had run back into the barn, and I could just see the flicker of her dress deep within the shadows.

"That's Brenda Stanley, the boss's wife."

"Cute."

"I'd rather put my pecker in a vise," said the old guy, still chewing on his mustache.

"Is that a professional opinion?"

But at that moment the ambulance came tearing up the driveway, lights flashing and the sirens scaring the horses off in the field. There's something about an ambulance that always makes it the most important object in any landscape. Like everything else just fades away.

I looked for Charlie. He was about ten feet behind me talking to another stable hand, the chubby guy, Paul Something, I had seen at the Parting Glass. Croteau took off his hat and began waving it around to get the attention of the ambulance driver. The ambulance drove across the grass, then pulled to a stop, and the siren died away into a melodic growl. Two guys jumped out and ran around back for a stretcher, while a third dashed into the barn. The doors slammed. The ambulance guys looked like they were trying to win a prize.

"There's no hurry," said Croteau. He said this rather casually, I thought.

The two ambulance guys jogged into the barn. They wore dirty white suits and white sneakers and they splashed through the mud as if it wasn't there.

Off in the fields I could see three men on horseback chasing after the big brown horse, which kept rearing up and shaking his head. It was kind of neat, like watching a movie. Charlie had ducked into the barn but I stayed outside with the help. Logan's son, Carl, had come out of the barn. He seemed pretty broke up and his face kept twitching as if he were exercising the muscles of his cheeks. The red-faced guy with the potbelly put his arm around him. He had gray whiskers and a gray beard and had high blood pressure written all over him. I stepped over to the old fellow who was eating his mustache. "Who's that?" I asked.

"Neil McClintock. He's the assistant trainer."

"You got a lot of people working here."

"Logan's got forty horses up here and another twenty down at Belmont. They take attention."

"Was that big brown horse a racehorse?"

"Nah, he's a riding horse. Usually he's the sweetest thing around. Must of gone crazy."

Two of the ambulance guys came out of the barn carrying the stretcher with a human-shaped lump under a red blanket. One hand was sticking out from under the blanket, and down the back of the hand was a wet stripe of blood, almost like a racing stripe. Everybody stared at the object on the stretcher. Logan's wife, Brenda Stanley, walked after it. If she had any tears, they were all internal. Beside her walked a tall hand-some man in a blue suit. He wasn't touching her but he walked close enough that he would be there to catch her if she fell. I guessed he was the foreman, Randall Hanks, the guy who Logan had said was poking his wife. He didn't seem partic-ularly grief-stricken. He had black hair that was graying at the temples and a nose that would have done a Barrymore proud.

"What's Randall Hanks like?" I asked the old guy.

"Ask him yourself, if you're so interested."

"You work for him?"

"I work for Logan."

"Not now you don't."

The guy gave me a look. "What's any of this to you anyhow?"

"I got a healthy curiosity. You know anything about Hanks poking Brenda Stanley?"

The old guy gave me another look, then spat out the tip of his mustache. "You're trouble," he said.

"You say the sweetest things."

He moved away from me like I might give him something that would make him itch. The ambulance guys had every-thing tucked away. They jumped in the front, revved the engine, then made a slow circle back toward the driveway.

They weren't in any hurry now. Down in the fields there was no sign of the crazy horse and his pursuers. Brenda Stanley was walking by herself toward the big ranch house. She had the straight back of someone who has spent a lot of time on show horses. The two globes of her ass under her white dress were a pretty sight even though she was too thin for my taste. Sunlight glittered on the glass roof of the greenhouse. I decided to take a peek inside the barn, partly to see where Charlie had gone and partly to check out the blood.

The inside of the barn seemed dark after the sunlight. It had a horse and hay smell. A few people were standing around up ahead of me but I couldn't make out who they were. On either side of the corridor were horse stalls, one with the top half of the door open and a big black horse sticking his neck over the top. What's happening? he seemed to say. He had a nervous, troubled look. I gave his nose a scratch or two, then moved on.

It was then that something unpleasant happened, but unpleasant in a small way. I mean, it was nothing like being run down by a horse. A rat popped out from between two bales of hay and went tearing right in front of me. I nearly tramped my muddy foot right down on top of its gray spaghetti tail. It was more the surprise than the rat itself that got to me, although I don't like rats. Still, I'm not the type to stand on a chair.

"Hey!" I shouted, and in that moment the rat disappeared.

"There's another one," someone said.

"They're all over the place," came another voice.

I looked around but didn't see any more rats. Ahead of me was the open door of a stall and from inside I could hear voices and maybe one was Charlie's. Just as I had nearly reached it, Donald Croteau stepped up from another direction and took a gander at me.

"Who are you?" he asked. It was not a voice full of sympathy and understanding stemming from my traumatic encounter with the rat.

"I had an appointment with Logan," I said.

"Didn't you see what happened? Why're you hanging around?" Croteau blocked my path to the stall, and I couldn't see past him.

"I've got a few questions. Anyway I only saw the results of what happened."

Croteau took another step toward me, making me step back. "What are you, some kind of thrill seeker? What's your name?"

"Vic Plotz."

"Plotz? What kind of name is that?" There was no friendly interest in this question, no genealogical curiosity.

"It's the sound a turd makes when it hits your face after falling from a great height. Plotz!"

Croteau got little white marks under his nose. He looked like he wanted to do something energetic with his hands.

Then Charlie appeared, apparently from nowhere. "Did you notify the police?" he asked.

Croteau turned, surprised. "Why, for an accident? I'll call the state police later. Who are you? Jesus, there're people popping up all over."

Charlie took out his identification. He loves identification, loves showing it, loves getting fancy little leather wallets in which to display it. And when he takes it out, he flicks open the cover with a little snap. It's probably something left over from when he was a cop.

Croteau took the wallet and peered over it for a moment. "A private detective? What the hell do I need you for? Does this wiseass belong to you?" Croteau jerked a thumb in my direction.

"He's my assistant," said Charlie.

"You both got five seconds to get off the property, otherwise I throw you off."

Guys like Croteau, no-nonsense guys with no sense of humor, give me psychosomatic hemorrhoids, it's what they call an hysterical symptom.

I was just beginning to make a you-and-who-else kind of remark when young Carl Logan interrupted.

"Wait a second, Don, I want to know why they're here."

The four of us were standing in the corridor of the barn. Some other people were nearby but I didn't really see who they were. I looked at Charlie, hoping he would take the ball and get professional. Croteau and Logan looked at him as well. Maybe that little porkpie hat gave him some kind of stature. I mean, why wear such a thing unless you've kissed the world of fashion goodbye? Like a monk's robe, maybe. Charlie tucked his ID back in his pocket. He can sometimes take on all the seriousness of a preacher. I can't do it myself. My lip curls or I start to grin. But Charlie puffs himself up and his eyes narrow. He takes off his glasses, then puts them back on again. He would have been great on the stage. Even his voice gets a little deeper. Authority, it's a mystery to me.

"Your father came to visit me yesterday," said Charlie, beginning one of his little lies. "He said he had evidence that someone was planning to murder him."

Carl Logan was clearly startled. He didn't strike his forehead with his fist or anything like that, but the surprise was just as obvious. His half brother, Donald Croteau, made a guffawing noise. "That's ridiculous!"

"Perhaps," said Charlie, "but he clearly felt himself in danger and he asked us to be here this morning. Now he is

dead before he could speak to us. Let me tell you, Mr. Croteau, if you do not call the police this very instant, then I'll
have to call them myself."

I felt proud. It was the kind of statement that needed only
a bunch of trumpets to set it off.

3

Logan's death made a big splash in the Sunday papers: Bronc Kicks Horse Owner to Death. It was a phrase that contained within it a slave-strikes-back kind of righteousness: the revenge of Spartacus. There were photographs of the horse and Logan, even a photo of the stall, and there was the sense that if you were foolish enough to own a bunch of horses, then you had to accept the occupational hazards. It was a punishment like a drunk falling off a bar stool or a doctor jabbing himself with a rusty needle. It had a karmic tidiness to it.

The article in the *Saratogian* described Logan as one of the biggest horse owners in New York State and said that last year his filly Wicked Girl had won the Schuylerville Stakes right here in Saratoga. Reading about how famous he was made me sorry that I hadn't asked for his autograph. I could have shown it to my granddaughter when she arrived in Saratoga to make my life miserable. There was a whole list of other wins, mostly in New York, but the Schuylerville Stakes was the biggest. I'd had money in that race but Wicked Girl hadn't been my choice. Maybe I would have picked her to show. Instead I had plopped down fifty bucks on a nag called Sweet Tooth that never got out of the gate. Somehow it made me dislike Logan.

The paper said he had been kicked to death by a horse named Triclops and that the body had been found in the horse's stall. It didn't say how crazy the horse had been or that it had tried to run me down. It didn't say that Logan thought his wife had wanted to kill him. Triclops wasn't a racehorse, or at least not anymore. The paper described him as a show horse belonging to Brenda Stanley.

My sense of the whole business was that Logan had had a suspicion which had come too late, like he had seen the shadow of the ax only when it was falling. The previous morning Charlie and I had hung around for a while after Carl Logan had called the state cops. The horse Triclops had been captured galloping across the battlefield. The park is popular with yuppies on mountain bikes and I hoped Triclops had given them a scare. He was brought back with half a dozen ropes on him and he was still hopping all over the place. The state guys poked around the stall and took lots of pictures. There was a ton of blood on the straw. Apparently Logan had gone into the stall and shut the door and then Triclops went crazy. Absolutely everybody felt obliged to say that Triclops had always been the sweetest horse they had ever known, like one of those guys who hauls off and shoots everyone in his office and the survivors all say: He always seemed so gentle! The only odd thing was that the rats kept popping up all over the place so you kept hearing people shout, There goes one! or There's a big mother! By one o'clock Charlie and I were out of there. On the road we passed the first of the reporters, a useless tub of lard from the *Saratogian* named Arnette Stroud. We both ducked so he wouldn't see us but maybe he recognized my Mercedes.

Anyway, it seemed to me that the business was over. Then I asked Charlie, "What about the thousand bucks?"

"We'll see about that," said Charlie.

There was a firmness to his tone which I didn't like.

Charlie's got a moral streak like a skunk's got a stripe. "Why don't we just divvy it up?" I asked. "Five hundred smackers would buy you a new roof."

"That wouldn't be honest, Victor."

"No, but it would be smart."

Charlie laughed, a kind of friendly chuckle. "That's always been my big problem. Smartness always comes second, if that."

So when Charlie called me late Sunday afternoon and said I had to come to his place right away, I knew that it concerned Logan. That's the trouble with carting around a cellular phone: people can always get you. What someone needs to invent is a little portable answering machine to go with it. Like I was standing in the Parting Glass sipping a Guinness with some of the lowlifes of my acquaintance and buzz-buzz Charlie had caught me.

"Charlie, I got a date."

"Tell her you won't be showing up."

"My romantic life means nothing to you."

"Aren't you the one who says you've got to make women suffer?"

"Does this concern Logan?"

"Just get out here."

· ● ·

So shortly past seven o'clock Sunday evening I'm driving out to Charlie's place on the lake. The sun had gone down but everything still looked a trifle pink. I drove out Union Avenue, past the racetrack, which was getting some fresh white paint, then the woods surrounding a big art colony, then over the bridge that spans the Northway: Route 87 shooting up to Montreal. The trees all looked excited by their newness and birds were doing pirouettes through the evening air. Spring makes me melancholy, and I was listening to Bill

Evans on the tape deck: "Body and Soul." The Mercedes seemed happy; it always is.

I felt bad about busting my date with the Queen of Softness. When you reach my age, you hate to give up a night of pleasure, and I could feel my pores yearning in the direction of her lunch counter. I love it when she leans across the Formica to give me a peck on the cheek. Then we would raid her big freezer for burgers and afterward we settle down to romance. Hot tubs and whiskey are supposed to be risky but I could think of worse ways to pop my heart.

To tell the truth, I was still bothered by the prospect of my granddaughter showing up in four weeks' time. Supposedly Susannah wanted to attend the dance school that the New York Ballet runs in Saratoga in July, but in the letter I received on Saturday she had also asked about Hebrew lessons and if the local temple had a youth society and if I cooked kosher or would mind if she did. It was all very sweet and earnest and I felt almost defective to find myself praying that a meteor would drop out of the skies over Chicago and bash her head in.

Let me say right now that I love religion. It's a great time occupier. If you don't watch TV, follow sports, read books or dig romance, then you might as well be religious. Catholics, Protestants, Jews, Muslims, Hindus, Buddhists—they are all wonderful people. I would be the last person to say they were short on inner resources. I mean, if they want to believe in a big gloved fist in the sky that wants to smack them around, I wish them pleasure in it. I'm quick enough with my own self-forgiveness so that I don't need to ask someone else to do it for me. Still, I'm crazy about religious people. I just don't want to live with them. As for Susannah cooking kosher, I think my stove would curl up and die. Oysters, lobsters, pork and dairy—that's my kind of soul food.

In her letter, Susannah had enclosed a seventh-grade picture of herself: a skinny girl with long brown hair in a ponytail and no chest. She had a kind of goofy smile and a bent nose that came right off her grandmother: my wife. I hadn't wanted to see that nose again. I had had my Saturday afternoon all planned and the wave of grief that swept over me hadn't been part of it. I don't even have any of my wife's pictures anymore, maybe I burned them, maybe Matt took them, but seeing Susannah's picture brought Sarah's face back to me again. Like when Sarah died she had nothing left but that nose. She had gotten thinner and thinner and the nose appeared to get bigger and bigger. I'd sit next to her hospital bed and stare at it and then she was dead and her nose seemed to get left behind. Matt doesn't have it; he's got my big toe of a nose. Sarah's nose jumped a generation and landed plop on Susannah's face. And this was the little girl who was going to come and live with me and make me eat kosher? Fat fuckin chance.

The Queen of Softness and me like to fool around with a camera. I put up the tripod, set the automatic timer and bingo, we're famous. I got a great shot of me shaving her pubic hair and another of us playing Elevator. I get these pictures blown up as eight-by-ten glossies, then I put them on the walls of my living room in the Algonquin so I can be happy when I am alone. You think I can leave these pictures up there when Susannah comes to visit? "What's that, Grampa, whatcha doin to that fat lady in the picture?" No way can I leave them on the wall. She'll probably even object to my cat: Moshe III.

So maybe that was why I was feeling melancholy as I drove out to Charlie's. Maybe I needed to make myself some Richard Pryor joke tapes to play instead of Bill Evans so I could switch to yuks at any time. Maybe what I don't like about the change of season is that it opens you up to the long

perspectives: other seasons, other lives. I liked my wife but
it's over. She got taken away. She's been dead for thirty years.
Only her nose lives on, that and the memories.

·   ●   ·

It was nearly dark when I got to Charlie's. He was out
in back, putzing over his tomato plants and batting at the
blackflies.

"You can still get a frost," I told him.

"No way," he said. "This year I got it beat. I ordered a
whole bunch of frost caps."

Last year he lost a dozen plants, all his little babies that
he had raised from seed under lights. He ended up buying
plants from a nursery, which was an insult to his green thumb.

"Give me a Jack Daniel's," I told him. "I'm feeling moody.
And put on a slinky black dress to cheer me up."

We went inside. He gave me the whiskey but ignored the
crack about the dress. "They'll be here any minute," he said.
The knees of his jeans were all muddy and his plaid shirt was
missing a button. He began unbuttoning his shirt as he stood
in the doorway of his bedroom. There were mud smudges on
his round red cheeks and a smudge on the lens of his glasses.

"They?"

"You'll see."

"Why so cagey?"

Charlie got all sparked up and his eyes got oversized. He
almost stamped his feet. "You got me into this, Victor! I told
you I had jury duty. I told you I had other cases. What can
I do with that thousand dollars? I can't give it back to a dead
man!"

"Maybe you need a whiskey yourself."

"Maybe I do."

After he changed his clothes, we sat down in the living
room. A cool breeze was blowing over the lake and Charlie

began to make a fire, crumpling up pages of the *Saratogian* and building a little tepee of sticks. I stared at the photograph of John Dillinger on the wall and wondered if he really had an eighteen-inch pecker that he had to strap to his leg. No wonder his girlfriend turned him in to the feds. After a few minutes I heard a car crunching across the gravel in the driveway.

The visitors were young Carl Logan and the assistant trainer, Neil McClintock, the bearded red-faced guy who looked like a stroke candidate huffing and puffing toward the big event. I don't know what it was about seeing them that made me realize Charlie was planning something unpleasant for me. Sometimes there is no one sneakier than the person who appears outwardly honest. We all shook hands and Charlie offered them whiskey. Young Logan didn't want anything. McClintock took a Budweiser. Both of them had long faces and looked like they could have used a tape of Richard Pryor jokes just like me.

"I want to hear again what my father said to this guy," Logan told Charlie when we were all seated. Logan was wearing khakis and a green chamois-cloth shirt. He was a nice-looking kid, and I had been prepared to like him. Now he was irritating me.

"My name's Vic," I said, "not 'this guy.' "

"Carl's upset," said McClintock, puffing up. "Can't you see his dad's been killed?" His face ran the color range from bright pink to scarlet.

Charlie cut in soothingly before I started bandying words with these bozos. "I'm sure Mr. Plotz will do everything he can. More whiskey, Vic?"

So I again told them about Bernard Logan's visit on Friday. If I had known that it was going to be so important, I would have videotaped it. McClintock kept trying to interrupt me—"Are you sure he said that?"—but young Logan shushed

him. McClintock couldn't sit still and was continually twitching and jerking, but you could tell he was crazy about the
kid by the way he kept glancing at him. He got feisty about
everything I said and seemed like a guy who sought out op-
portunities to lose his temper. McClintock's salt-and-pepper
beard and mustache made the redness of his face brighter
than it really was. He had a beer belly and he kept stroking
it as he listened, like he was going to give birth to a quarter
keg. Burp!

"Did my father say anything in particular about this letter
he'd found?" asked Carl.

"Nope, just that he'd found one. It was supposed to in-
criminate the two of them somehow. The main thing, as far
as your dad was concerned, was overhearing Brenda Stanley
and Randall Hanks on the telephone."

"What about the rattrap?" asked McClintock.

"He said it was actually a cage. I don't know, you have
much trouble with rats out there?"

Young Logan looked puzzled. He had mussed curly black
hair that some young girl probably loved to run her hands
through. "Not usually, but this weekend they seem to be
overrunning the place. It's like a plague."

"Tell us about this Brenda Stanley," Charlie said. He put
another log on the fire, then stood back as the sparks shot
up.

"My dad married her about eight years ago. I was away
at boarding school at the time. I came home for Christmas
and there she was."

"A present from Santa," I said.

"She fucking seduced him is what I think," said Mc-
Clintock. "She wanted his money and just took aim at him.
She must have thought that he owned the whole place by
himself."

"And didn't he?" asked Charlie.

"The farm was owned jointly by my parents," said Carl. "My mother died when I was nine years old. She'd been married before to a man named Croteau, and they had one kid: Donald. He's twelve years older than me. My father always resented him and was jealous of Donald's father. He's dead now as well, a car accident. My mother was afraid that when she died my dad would just kick Donald out. He was at Hamilton and doing badly—"

"Too many parties," interrupted McClintock. He shook his head as if parties were the source of half the world's trouble.

"So my mother changed her will to leave eighty percent of her share in the farm to Donald and twenty percent to me, meaning that Donald now has forty percent and I've got ten percent. Donald has a house on the property, owns horses and trains them. My father tried to buy him out, but Donald has always refused to sell."

"Did he like your father?" Charlie asked.

"He liked to make him grind his teeth," said McClintock. "When Logan's first wife was dying, Logan refused to visit her in the hospital. I don't know why. Maybe it upset him too much. Or maybe he just didn't care about her. Donald took a leave from college and stayed with her. Then when she died, he quit college and had that place built out on the farm. Sometimes I think he stayed just to keep reminding Logan of how he had treated his mother."

"How does Donald get along with Brenda Stanley?" asked Charlie.

"He despises her," said McClintock, "and I wouldn't be surprised if Logan didn't marry her partly to get at him."

"I don't believe that," said Carl.

McClintock drained his beer and set the empty on the coffee table. "Brenda likes men to look at her, she flirts a lot, maybe most of it's pretty harmless. A few years ago she made a pass at Donald and I thought he was going to hit her. She just laughed."

"Does she stand to inherit anything?" asked Charlie.

"That's part of the problem," said McClintock. "It was written into their marriage contract. She gets fifty percent of Logan's half of the farm."

"And I get the other fifty percent," said Carl.

"Looks like you folks will have to learn to love each other," I said. "Maybe you should buy a hot tub."

It seemed like a good idea but no one paid any attention. Both Carl Logan and McClintock were leaning forward on the couch with their elbows on their knees. The fire snapped and crackled and occasionally Charlie would give it a poke. I sipped my whiskey, giving it little liquid kisses. A big moon was coming up over the lake.

"So now," said Charlie, "Donald Croteau will have forty percent of the farm, Carl will have thirty-five percent and Brenda will have twenty-five percent. And did she really have an insurance policy on him?"

"A big one," said Carl. "Three hundred thousand. She says that my dad took it out for her himself."

"And I say she's lying," said McClintock. "He already had another one with Carl as beneficiary. Why take out a second policy to benefit someone he hated?" McClintock had a big red nose pocked with old acne scars. If he lay on his back, it would become the Mount Vesuvius on the Scottish landscape of his face. Each time he got angry the nose seemed in danger of popping.

"Logan said he liked her," I chimed in.

"Not anymore," said McClintock. "She was trying to humiliate him. I can't imagine he would have taken out a second insurance policy and made her the beneficiary. She must have done it, then tricked him into signing it."

"How long has Hanks been foreman?" asked Charlie.

"Almost a year," said Carl. The tone of his voice indicated that he had little use for Hanks. "He was hired in June, just before I graduated from college."

McClintock made a snorting noise. "She started fucking Hanks right at the beginning. I caught them once in the barn. She likes to wear these long skirts and you know for certain that she's got nothing on beneath them. Hanks had her spread across a hay bale. I was looking for something, I don't remember what, maybe a bridle. I barged right in without thinking. She just grinned at me, didn't even have the decency to look embarrassed."

"What about Hanks?" asked Charlie.

"He started yelling at me to get out, like being foreman made him think he owned the place and that included the boss's wife." McClintock snorted again.

"Does she strike you as someone who might kill her husband?" asked Charlie. He stood up to get McClintock another beer, and while he was out in the kitchen he also grabbed some crackers and cheese. From the cupboards came rustling, banging noises.

McClintock raised his voice. "Sure, she stood to inherit a bundle."

But Carl wasn't so positive. "I've always liked her and she's been friendly to me. And my dad liked her for a long time even though he knew she was unfaithful. They'd stay up late at night in the living room, drinking whiskey and talking. I'd hear them laughing sometimes until four a.m., right up until when it was time to exercise the horses. She's great at that. She loves riding. But my dad didn't like this business with Randall Hanks. It was different from her other affairs, more serious, and Hanks started throwing his weight around. He tangled with Donald one day and Donald took a swing at him. The next thing I knew they were both rolling in the dirt."

"I had to break it up," said McClintock. "I thought they'd kill each other, but afterward they came to some understanding, some kind of crooked deal, if you ask me."

"Why didn't your father fire Hanks?" asked Charlie, returning from the kitchen with a tray of stuff.

"It's only been in the past few months that it's gotten worse," said Carl. "Then Brenda said that if Hanks went, she'd leave as well. My dad was furious about that. I don't know how people accommodate themselves to things, why he didn't fire him anyway. My dad shut up and Brenda moved to another bedroom—that was about a month ago. For a while she and Hanks tried to be more subtle, but a couple of times recently I've seen them sneaking off. He's got an apartment that adjoins the bunkhouse. As for her killing my dad, I find that hard to believe, but maybe I'd have a hard time imagining anybody killing anybody. I bet Hanks could do it. No, I have trouble imagining even that. Right now the whole thing looks like an accident. There's no proof that he was murdered."

"What about what he told me?" I said.

"That still doesn't constitute proof," said Charlie.

"The horse belonged to your stepmother?" I asked.

"It was her favorite horse, a jumper," said Carl. "She'd use it in shows. I think she rode it nearly every day."

"What did the state police find?" asked Charlie.

"Nothing to prove my dad wasn't killed by Triclops. The wounds on his head, the blood on the horse's hooves . . ."

"Is there going to be an autopsy?" asked Charlie.

"I don't know," said Carl. "I mean, if he was kicked to death, what's the point?"

Charlie poured himself some more whiskey and stirred the ice around with his little finger. "Just to see if there is any other kind of wound. When's the funeral?"

"Tuesday out of Bethesda Episcopal Church in Saratoga."

Nobody said anything for a moment. Charlie began cutting slices off a big chunk of yellow cheese and neatly placing the individual slices on some Triscuits, which he had arranged in three rows. I took a couple crackers just to disrupt his pattern. The only noise was the fire and the sound of chewing. Maybe we were all pondering the big imponderables: death and the great unknown. Maybe we were just letting our food settle. The reflection of the moon on the lake made a big white splotch. McClintock was scratching his beard like he had beard mites.

"Let's say Brenda Stanley and Randall Hanks had nothing to do with your dad's death," said Charlie. "Is there anyone else who might have a motive for killing him?"

McClintock and Carl Logan glanced at each other. Maybe it was guilt, maybe it was just shared knowledge. McClintock took a swig of his Budweiser.

"For instance," said Charlie, "with Logan dead it seems that Donald has a controlling interest in the farm. That's not a bad motive. Would he have any other reason?"

McClintock got red in the face again. "Donald and Frankie Faber were cheating Logan in some way. Logan got wind of it."

"Faber's the trainer?" asked Charlie.

"Yeah. He's down at Belmont right now."

"He's your boss?" I asked McClintock.

"Not really. I mean, technically he's my boss but I work mostly with Carl."

"I've got a few horses of my own," said Carl. "Faber works with Donald and my dad. Of course, down at Belmont the horses are all in the same barn. I mean, it's all Battlefield Farms. Neil's assistant trainer, and if Donald or Frankie Faber has a job for him, then he does it, unless he's involved with one of my horses. Faber chooses all the mounts, picks the races, deals with the jockeys' agents."

"What kind of person is he?" asked Charlie.

This seemed a difficult question, because neither of them leapt in to answer it. Carl began to break apart a cracker; McClintock returned to scratching his beard.

"He's Donald's man," said Carl at last. "Donald hired him about five years ago."

"Your father didn't object?"

"No," said Carl. "I mean, Faber's a good trainer and he's done well for us, at least until recently. He's an active guy and he's got a lot of contacts. When Donald brought him around I don't think there was anything against him. I was away at college at the time: Cornell."

"I've never had any problem with him," said McClintock. "We're not chummy but at least he's professional. He'd been out on the West Coast before coming here. He's sly and can be a real operator at the track, but at least I thought he was our operator and not someone else's."

"What did you mean that he's done well for you until recently?" asked Charlie.

"We run a lot of our horses in claiming races," said McClintock, "and we pick up horses in claiming races as well. I don't know how much you know about it, but claiming races are a tricky form of gambling. You collect a bunch of nags all worth sixty-two fifty or ten grand or even more, you put them together in a race, and the fact they're worth the same amount makes you think they're more or less equal, because once the race starts another trainer can buy any of the horses as long as he's got the hard cash."

"There's no fraud involved," said Logan, "or at least not usually, but there's a certain amount of subterfuge. If you've got a horse that's been running in sixty-two-fifty claiming races and he suddenly gets a lot better, then you can put him in a ten-grand race . . ."

"Or," said McClintock, "you can hide how well he's

doing and keep him in the sixty-two-fifty. Maybe you put bandages on his ankles to suggest tendon problems or maybe you add blinkers or work him out at home rather than down at the track, because if another trainer knows you've got a valuable horse, he'll claim him away from you. It's a gamble, right? Well, Frankie Faber was pretty good at it. He had a good eye. He won quite a few races and he claimed some good horses."

"Why do you say 'was'?" asked Charlie, always on top of his grammar and tenses.

"Recently," said Carl, "Frankie's been losing some good horses. He's put a couple of our top horses in cheap races and they got snatched from us."

"Sometimes you can't do anything about it," said McClintock. "You just have a streak of bad luck. But these horses should have never been in those races in the first place, and Logan got suspicious."

"Why should he do that?" asked Charlie.

"Well, if you put a thirty-thousand-dollar horse in a ten-thousand-dollar race," said McClintock, "and you tip off the right party, then it might be worth, say, ten grand to you."

"And you think Faber did that?"

"I think he did something like that."

"Could he do it without Croteau knowing?" asked Charlie.

Logan and McClintock didn't say anything for a moment. They seemed like fairly honest guys who were surprised by the dark corners of the world. I ate some more crackers.

"I don't see how Donald couldn't have known about it," said Carl at last.

"It's just been in the past week that any of us really thought something funny might be going on," said Mc-Clintock. "We lost our third good horse last Monday at Belmont, a beauty of a filly named Margaret's Revenge. We were all set to run her in some stakes races and she goes for ten grand."

"Did she win the race?" I asked.

"By about ten lengths," said McClintock, "and she wasn't even breezin'. We got the purse but it was nothing compared to losing the horse."

"So Logan thought that Croteau and Faber were cheating him?"

Young Logan looked uncertain. "I don't know what he knew, but he was suspicious. He couldn't believe that Faber had lost Margaret's Revenge accidentally. She was a great horse."

"What could he have done if he knew they were cheating?" I asked.

"Conspiracy to defraud," said Charlie. "They'd be out of the racing association and could face jail as well."

"I can't see Croteau losing three of our best horses for a kickback," said Carl. "It's not as if he's broke or anything. He's got forty percent of Battlefield Farms."

"But if Croteau was cheating your father," said Charlie, "and your father knew about it and planned to go to the association, then Croteau might want to shut his mouth."

"But how?" said Carl. "I mean, my father was kicked to death by a horse. Wasn't he?"

"Where'd all those rats come from?" asked Charlie.

Carl Logan and McClintock both scratched their heads: two monkeys with nothing but question marks in their brains. Their lives had taken a downward turn into confusion and all they could do was rile up the dandruff.

"Anybody else with a motive?" asked Charlie.

"No," said Carl. "I mean, the people who work for us are all old-timers."

"What about you?" I asked. "You get half of your dad's

share in the farm, plus a chunk of insurance money. You got a good reason to see him dead."

"Hey," said McClintock. "Watch it." McClintock put his hands on his knees and looked tough.

"Or if not you," I said to Logan, "then your buddy here: Mr. Red-in-the-Face. He's looking out for your best interests and decides to kill your old man before Brenda Stanley or Donald Croteau robs him blind."

McClintock had turned scarlet and I thought he might have a stroke right on top of the cheese.

"Neil wouldn't do anything like that," said Carl. "That's crazy. He liked Dad."

"It's been done before," said Charlie in a friendly, soothing voice. "If we are looking for motives, then you and McClintock have one, no matter how small or implausible. It's still possible that your dad's death was an accident, but the fact that he talked to Victor about murder can't be ignored."

Carl looked depressed and McClintock looked cranky. I figured they wanted to go someplace and mope. But they had bigger plans.

"That's why we wanted to talk to you, Charlie," said Logan. "My dad gave you some money. I'd like to give you some more. I want you to come out to the farm and see what's going on."

"I have a problem," said Charlie. "I've got jury duty starting tomorrow. Maybe it will last a day or so, maybe it will last a month."

The pig, he actually sounded pleased that he had jury duty.

"But who can we get?" asked Logan.

It didn't hit me right away but Logan's tone was suspiciously smooth, like cat fur on a brick. Then I realized that all three were looking at me. "Hey," I said, "I'm not a detective. I'm an entrepreneur. What about all those irons I got in the fire?"

"Let them cool," said Charlie. "You can ask questions and poke around."

"I don't have a license and I don't have a gun. I'd only get in trouble." I had the feeling that I was sliding down a steep metal roof as the Queen of Softness leaned from a dormer window and watched me go.

"Not having a license has never stopped you from doing anything," said Charlie. "And you don't need a gun."

"After all," said Logan, "you were the one who first talked to my father."

"It's like it's your responsibility," said McClintock. He did something with his mouth that resembled a grin. This was absolutely the first trace of humor I'd seen in the man.

Charlie smiled and sipped some whiskey. The fire was reflected in his bifocals and the flames seemed to dance across his eyes. Sometimes I think he is positively evil.

4

$\mathbf{M}$onday morning I had to get up early in order to plague my tenants, add another wrinkle to their wash-and-wear lives. I got four duplexes which I rent out for big bucks during the five weeks of racing season and moderate bucks for the rest of the year. But from this particular tenant I'd recently been getting no bucks at all. Like since March he had been a charity case: my charity. I could have walloped myself over the head for renting to him at all. I should have known better when I saw his Harley: the Hog, he called it. But his girlfriend had these big breasts with tattoos all over them and somehow they befogged my vision. I couldn't stand the thought of those breasts going to some other landlord. Now not only was the guy not paying the rent but he was also busting up the furniture and his pit bull was pissing on the rug. Worse, he made so much noise playing his old Elvis records that the nice upstanding family in the other half of the duplex had moved out. Since then the ker had been after me to rent the other half to some friends his. I told him that hell would have to freeze over first and he asked me if I'd ever heard of squatter's rights and occupation being nine-tenths of the law, etc. This was the impasse to which we had come.

It was six-thirty in the morning and I was standing outside

his front door, actually my front door. The duplex is on High Rock Avenue only a couple of blocks from my place on Broadway. I had parked out in front, right behind my tenant's Harley, which was black with flames painted on the front fender to make it look cool. Beneath the Harley was a puddle of oil. For these occasions I often carry a cane. Not only does it make me seem frail and the sort of guy that only a brute would pick on, it also gives me a weapon. The end of the cane is a big solid knot of wood, and with this I proceeded to hammer on the door. The pit bull responded with a frantic hysteria which warmed my heart and after a minute or so the woman opened up. She's called Puma. I don't know if that's a first name or a last name. She wasn't quite bare-breasted but she might as well have been. Her garment was perhaps called a pajama halter. The two halves enclosed her nipples like a pair of slingshots holds a pair of stones. Her breasts were as heavy as bowling balls and had vines, tree trunks, monkeys, snakes and parrots tattooed across them in about ten colors.

She opened the door and stood there a moment. "What you looking at?" she said.

"Trying to see if I can find Tarzan. He was a childhood hero of mine."

"Did you come here just to glom my tits?"

"I want to talk to your old man. Make it snappy. I'm on a schedule."

Puma shut the door and I waited. Her old man's name was Ernie Flako, which seemed a poor sort of name for someone whose role model was Attila the Hun.

Ernie yanked open the door. He was wearing only undershorts but he had so much hair on his chest and arms that he seemed fully dressed. He has a lot of obligatory physical stuff: big beer belly, tattoos of witches riding the whirlwind, gold earring, black bushy beard, black pony-tail, love and hate tattoos on his knuckles, gold tooth. In his own way he was dressed as correctly as a Wall Street lawyer.

"You have two days to move out of here," I told Ernie, "otherwise I break you like a pane of glass."

Ernie attached his meathooks to the lapels of my gray suit and raised me off the ground. Instead of being gainfully employed like most people, he lifts weights. I'm one hefty mass of flesh and the only way I'll see two hundred pounds again is when the worms slim me down in my coffin. Like the song says, I'm built for comfort, I'm not built for speed. Ernie is four inches taller than me. He lifted me up to eye level, then searched around for something to say. He's a pre-verbal kind of guy. Language for him is just beyond the next evolutionary stepping-stone. While he was thinking, I set the point of my cane against his bare foot, and he set me down again, not too gently I might add.

"Two days, Ernie," I said. "I'd hate to see you get hurt."

"You and who else?" he asked.

It was not a remark that made a lot of sense. "I don't know, Ernie. Maybe your mother, maybe Puma. Surely there must be someone else who cares if you get hurt."

I let him ponder that as I walked back to my car. As I was driving away, my Mercedes—I don't know how it happened—bumped Ernie's Harley so that it toppled over onto the grass. In my rearview mirror, I saw Ernie running down the steps toward his Harley just like a mother might run toward a toddler who has fallen into a bonfire. It showed he had a heart after all.

After having completed this good work, I drove out Lake Avenue toward Battlefield Farms. The sun was not too high

over the Green Mountains and the robins were out rustling
up the worms. Blue sky, warm spring day, I felt like a kid
again.

• ● •

Charlie had set me three tasks. One, I needed to find proof
that Bernard Logan's death wasn't an accident. Two, I needed
to find out what kind of guy Logan had been. Three, I had
to throw my weight around and draw attention to myself. It
was that last task that cheered me the most, because I'm the
kind of guy who needs a stage. I like to stand at the footlights
belting out a song, just like Eddie Cantor singing "Swannee."

If I'd had any brains as a kid, I would have been an actor,
but to tell the truth, until the death of my wife, I was a pretty
modest guy, a guy who felt you got ahead by keeping your
nose clean. Was I far off base or what? I'd measure rich guys
for their suits and speak in a purr, always nodding my head
so I had a constant crick in my neck. I'd get down on my
knees and run the measuring tape up into their groins and
make little chalk marks on their sleeves, and whisper at them
like I felt they were one of the most fortunate guys in God's
green acre and why they hadn't gotten the Nobel Prize was
a mystery to me.

It wasn't a matter of being deferential, it was a matter of
being a doormat. My wife's death changed that. I must have
been a real jerk. Playing by the rules doesn't let you off anything. Like death sends down its fishhook into this great mass
of flounder and who it snags is just somebody's bad luck.
Hey, big mouth or modest, we all got to die. So after my
wife's funeral I go back to Schultz's Men's Furnishings and
maybe I'd had a few whiskeys too many and some lawyer
type stares down his nose at me and asks about his pinstripe
and I tell him it looks like whipped cream on a turd. Schultz

wasn't a bad fellow but he couldn't take too much of that and after a few months I was gone.

Why Charlie wanted me to draw attention to myself was that if Logan had actually been murdered, then the killer must be feeling pretty smug that he or she had pulled off this business so easily. My huffing and puffing around the property was meant to throw a scare into the guilty party.

Now, over the years, I have developed a pretty healthy ego. After all, I'm big, intelligent, and handsome and I got a sex life like Kuwait's got oil. But the trouble with this type of ego is that I'm too prone to believe that everything is going to turn up daisies. I'm too prone to believe I'm going to get my own way. If I think something, then I mostly believe it is the right thing to think just because I'm thinking it. The idea never occurs to me that if my job is to throw my weight around, then I might end up with a broken head. Trusting and innocent, that's me.

I got out to Battlefield Farms a little after seven and parked the Mercedes in the lot by the greenhouse. You might think I was a tad early but these were horse people and they tend to be out on the track exercising their equity by five a.m. Seems crazy to me. Like a farmer and his cows. Why can't the farmer teach his cows to be milked at noon and midnight, a nice civilized hour? I bet the milk would even taste better.

I climbed out of my car and locked up. Several horses were being cooled down, walked around in circles by the hot walker. Several other horses were being heated up, galloping around the training track. There were roosters crowing and a goat was making goat noises. A couple of long-tongued golden retrievers bounced up and proceeded to get dog spit on my knees. I saw the old guy in the blue jeans get up, who I had talked to on Saturday, brushing down a horse. And I saw the chubby guy, Paul Something, leading a mare back to the stall. These guys saw me as well but they didn't wave or otherwise indicate that without me their lives were meaningless. I sauntered over to the training track. Everything was so peaceful and pretty that it seemed impossible to believe that this was a place where murder could screw up the ambience.

I leaned up against the fence. Donald Croteau and another guy were about twenty feet away, timing a horse, but I paid them no mind. They'd see me soon enough. About seven horses were still on the track, some going slow, some going fast, straight out with the rider bent down low and working. Their hooves in the soft dirt made a happy drumming sound. I'm the kind of guy that doesn't trust beauty. Like it's a distraction. You stand there staring at the posies, thinking how pretty they are, and then *whap*, something smacks you from behind. When my wife was dying, the doctors gave her morphine to take her mind off her troubles: beauty is like that. The big distraction. But a racehorse—I defy you to find an ugly one. I mean, even the bad ones are beautiful. And the good ones look exquisite. Every one of them can be traced back to two Arab stallions and a Turk that the Brits bred to their own mares over two hundred years ago.

Trainers and the guys that know the business talk about conformation, which is how well the horse is put together: ratios of legs to back and if the horse toes out and what his knees look like. It's not something a bozo like me will notice unless I compare the nags in a sixty-two-fifty claiming race to the horseflesh that runs in the Travers Stakes. But even those sixty-two-fifty nags are pretty. What amazes me about horse racing is that you have all this classy apparatus just so some old retired fart can place a two-dollar bet at Belmont. It's like the Queen of England bending down to do the dirty with someone like me. What fuels it, I guess, are the egos of the owners and how they get caught up in the razzmatazz and get their rocks off parading around the paddock and being looked at by the hoi polloi. It costs at least fifteen grand a year to keep a horse in training, so you figure someone like Logan was easily laying out a minimum of half a million. So he won the fuckin Schuylerville stakes and some other races and he brings in some bucks by taking care of some other folks' horses—I tell you, you'd stand a better chance striking it rich on the Lotto.

Brenda Stanley was cantering along on a big chestnut stallion. She kept her back as straight as a chimney and the saddle barely patted her bottom. She's got short blond hair that flapped about her ears as she rode. While not skinny, she was thin. No love handles or chunks of meat to lift: a beef-jerky kind of girl. She would have been a beautiful woman with forty more pounds on her. But even thin she was cute. I remembered what McClintock had said about seeing her getting fucked on a hay bale and it made me grip the rail of the fence a little more tightly. She wore green riding pants and a little green jacket over a white blouse. When she passed me again, she was standing in the stirrups to slow the horse down. There was a brash sort of grace to her manner, a casualness, and as she rode by Croteau she raked her eyes over him. Then she turned the horse's head toward the gate. When she reached it, I was there to say hi.

"Ms. Stanley," I said, "I wonder if I could have a word with you about a sensitive matter." I bent my lips into a smile that made me look forthright and honest.

Brenda reined in her horse and stared down at me. Her head was about four feet above my own, which gave her, I felt, an unfair advantage. The chestnut stallion sniffed in my direction as if it wanted to nibble my lapels. Brenda's expression indicated that her heart was not beating fast, nor had she decided that I was the new Romeo in her life. She looked like a lover of gourmet food faced with a platter of Cheez Whiz.

"What about?" she said.

"I'd like to talk to you about your husband."

"He's dead."

She turned the horse's head to get around me and I took hold of his bridle. This was a mistake. She was carrying a little riding crop and she slashed at me with it. I stepped back, letting go of the horse and rubbing my arm.

"Never touch my horse," she said casually, then she put her heels to the horse's flanks and trotted off.

The word for all this was "inauspicious." I watched Brenda Stanley ride off in the direction of the barn, then I walked after her. I saw Croteau looking in my direction, but he didn't make any other motion, and I looked away. It wasn't time to talk to him yet.

As I walked toward the barn, a kid I had seen on horse-back Saturday morning came hurrying toward me carrying a white plastic bag. He was young enough to be still in high school. He wore a blue denim shirt and a green down vest. He held the bag away from him as if it were dangerous.

"What d'you got in the bag?" I asked.

"Rats."

"Dead or alive?"

"These are dead but there're plenty of live ones around." He had a heavily freckled face and reddish-brown hair, a skinny kid but muscular all the same.

"I'll give you ten bucks for every rat you can catch alive."

"You serious?"

"Never more," I said.

"What do I catch them with?"

"That's up to you, maybe a butterfly net, maybe a piece of cheese."

"What d'you want them for?"

"It's a scientific experiment. You on or not?"

"Sure, I guess so."

"Here's ten bucks to cement the deal. Shake." He took the money and we shook hands. He had a strong handshake for a kid. I nodded to him and proceeded on to the barn.

Brenda was rubbing liniment onto the legs of her big chestnut stallion when I finally caught up to her. She was outside one of those white shed rows with green trim. She didn't look up at me.

"We were rudely interrupted," I said.

She continued massaging the horse's legs. It looked like fun.

"I was wondering if you could explain to me how your husband was kicked to death by a horse that by all accounts was a perfectly happy-go-lucky hunk of horseflesh."

She slowly turned her head in my direction. She had blue eyes of the sort that look sharp and pointed. At the moment they looked angry. If I was a personnel director in the business of hiring sweet Sunday-school teachers, I'm afraid she wouldn't get the job. She'd scare the kiddies. She'd scare even the parents.

"What business is it of yours?" she asked.

"I'm just a humble workingman trying to wrap my corpulence around a paycheck. Consequently, it has become my business or I have made it so. How come Triclops kicked your husband to death?"

Brenda Stanley stood up. She was my height although half my weight. She looked pretty cute in her little green suit. Her short blond hair fell right to the line of her jaw. Her eyes took on a glimmer of understanding. "You a cop?"

"Private."

"Who's paying you?"

"Your stepson."

"Donald? I can't believe it."

"The other one: Carl."

"Carl's paying you to investigate me?"

"Not necessarily you, just to investigate. Can we get back to me asking the questions now?"

But she wasn't quite ready for that. Brenda marched off toward another stall about ten feet away, leaving me, presumably, in charge of her horse. The horse and I looked at each other. There was no love lost. I didn't even have any spare carrots to give it. "Dog meat, dog meat," I whispered in his ear, but he was a one-day-at-a-time kind of creature and I couldn't rattle him.

Brenda looked into the stall and called out, "Randall, will you come out here a minute? I've got a problem."

Randall Hanks came hurrying through the door. Although he was wearing work clothes, they were neatly pressed. I don't know about you, but I've always been deeply suspicious of anyone with creases in their Levi's. He had a handsome face, like a porterhouse steak with dark brown eyes. He wore a quizzical, how-may-I-be-of-service kind of look.

"That man over there says he's a private detective," Brenda said, as if I were claiming I could do cartwheels or bat .500 in postseason play. "He says he's been hired to investigate Bernard's death. I don't like it."

Randall Hanks's response was perfectly straightforward. "Out," he said, walking toward me. "Off the property."

In a moment they were standing on either side of me. What with the big chestnut stallion we made quite a crowd. I tried on a little smile but it was no good. I work and work on these smiles, spend hours sweating in front of the mirror, and still nobody believes them.

"I've been employed by Carl Logan," I said. "He owns

thirty-five percent of Battlefield Farms. That being the case, you have no right to kick me off the property."

Hanks took hold of my lapels. "Want to see me?"

It occurred to me that this was the second time in a single morning that my lapels had been grabbed. It made me think I was living too close to the edge.

"Are you Randall Hanks?" I asked. "I mean, am I face to face with the real Mr. Hanks?" This close to him I could see that his black hair had some kind of spray on it to keep it in place. A dapper guy.

"What of it?" said Hanks, holding me a little tighter.

"Then you are the very person who Mr. Bernard Logan told me on Friday afternoon was planning to murder him."

If I had been burning hot, Hanks could not have let me go any faster. Even the horse stepped away.

"What do you mean by that?" asked Brenda.

"And you're his wife, right? Brenda Stanley? Your husband told me you were all set to bump him off. How lucky I am to catch you both together. Tell me, how did you manage it?"

"We never did anything to him," said Hanks. "What the hell you talking about?"

For all that he was over six feet tall and had a handsome puss, Hanks struck me as no Einstein. Understanding for him was like the red caboose disappearing in the distance as he jogged his weary way along the train tracks. When he asked a question, he stood there with his face wide open like a kid waiting to catch a ball. Brenda Stanley was different. She had speedy eyes and I had the sense that she had figured out my manner pretty quick. Since she had a good brain, she didn't require one in Hanks as well. He was just a prick with a man attached. I decided to come straight with them.

"My name's Vic Plotz. I work for Charlie Bradshaw, a

private investigator in Saratoga. Around noon on Friday, Bernard Logan showed up in our office wanting to hire Charlie. He said he had definite proof that the two of you were planning to murder him in order to cash in on an insurance policy and to take over a big chunk of the farm. He left a retainer of a thousand bucks and told us to be out here at ten-thirty Saturday morning, when he would show us the proof concerning your conspiracy. We got here only to find him dead. We have now been hired by Carl Logan to determine whether his father's death was accidental or intentional: that is, murder."

Through this little speech Hanks's face had been steadily losing color. "Jesus! Murder? Why in the world . . ."

"Be quiet, Randall," interrupted Brenda.

While Hanks's facial muscles were doing acrobatic flips, Brenda Stanley bore no expression at all.

"What specific proof did my husband say that he had?"

"I would prefer not to divulge it."

"And why did we want him dead?"

"It's no secret that the two of you are having an affair. He also said that you had taken out a big insurance policy on him."

"He took out that policy himself and gave it to me."

"That's not what he told me. Why should he do that, considering you been having this illicit fling?"

"Brenda, let me kick his ass outta here," said Hanks, slipping back into the mood in which he felt most comfortable.

Brenda put a hand on Hanks's chest. "Take care of Velvet Trouble, will you? I think I better talk to this man by myself."

Hanks looked at her first with surprise, then suspicion. He was one of those big dummies who have no control over their faces. Like he could have made a fortune in a college art class displaying the ten basic emotions to undergraduates. Brenda took my arm and walked me away.

"Nice guy," I said conversationally. "Have you taught him to read yet?"

"I love him, Mr. . . ."

"Plotz. It's onomatopoeic. Picture it as a mud fight. Plotz, plotz! How come good-looking women like you always go for guys with Stone Age brains? If you ask me, Mr. Hanks is still wrassling with the evolutionary ladder."

"Who we love or don't love never seems a matter of choice. I had great respect for my husband but I never loved him. I tried for years. We had wonderful times together, but I couldn't love him."

"Then Mr. Cro-Magnon comes bopping along in his leopard suit and flicks your switch."

"That's about it, Mr. Plotz."

"Call me Vic, we're all friends here. You can rest your head on my shoulder if you'd like."

She smiled. "I don't think it would be appropriate."

I was struck by how she had decided to get along with me, and it seemed that Hanks's wish to throw me off the property and Brenda's newly discovered friendly manner both derived from the same source: an attempt to deal with a threat. You can bet your boots that I was won over by her tactics more than by his. Still, I knew that it was something phony, merely a strategy. Like we weren't about to hang around her kitchen swapping chowder recipes. She would never, sad to say, be a true friend.

"Tell me about your husband," I asked. "What kind of guy was he?"

She gave me an expression that indicated that she meant to be frank, looking at me directly as she lowered her head so that I could see the whites beneath her pupils. She was a sly one. We walked along the shed row. Grooms were tending to the horses, rubbing them up and brushing them down. Several looked at me curiously, knowing I was there because Logan had been killed. There was a big oak tree that we were walking toward. The sun was still low in the east and there was mist over the river. Up here in Saratoga County the Hudson River is still a child.

"When we were first married I thought of Bernard as my best friend. He cared deeply about me and tried to make sure I was happy. But I don't think Bernard really understood friendship, never believed in it. He had many acquaintances, even some chums, but no real friends, and so while he loved me and liked me, he also felt uncomfortable with me. At the time, I was in my late twenties and he was thirty years older. He had medical problems and sex was difficult for him. In the past few years we had stopped having sex altogether."

"Wasn't that because you were seeing other guys?"

"You are confusing your cause with your effect, Mr. Plotz. I saw the other guys, as you call them, because of what Bernard wasn't able to do himself. He never really minded as long as I didn't take them seriously."

"And then Brickbrain came along."

"You're so kind."

"How did Logan react to it?"

"He put up with it at first just as he had with the others, but then, when he understood its seriousness, he became very angry. For the first time he had the sense that I had betrayed him. He told me to break it off. And I made a mistake. I told him I would, but I was lying. When he realized that Randall and I were still seeing each other, he became furious."

I have never understood that euphemism for fucking: seeing each other. It makes it an eye thing, instead of a body thing. When I'm seeing the Queen of Softness, my eyes are usually shut.

"What does Hanks do as foreman?" I asked.

"Basically he runs the farm, takes care of the maintenance. There's a hayfield and constant mending of the fences. He does everything that wouldn't be done by the trainer. He's good at it. Bernard used to do most of that himself, but increasingly over the past few years he had lost interest in the farm and became more withdrawn. The impotence bothered him, and he was also having trouble with his heart. Donald told me that when Bernard was younger he'd been very active, sexually. It's one of the many things that Donald holds against him. Bernard's change, his increasing indifference to the farm, I thought was connected to his own sexual problems and sense of frailty. This is somewhat speculative. You see, Bernard was very private. If he had some physical problem, he would never tell me. It again had to do with not understanding the nature of friendship. He shared nothing of the deeper part of himself. To say that he was withdrawing from life seems overly dramatic, but life itself, the actual day-to-day work of it, didn't excite him as much. Four years ago he had that greenhouse built. He spent more and more time with his orchids and tropical plants."

"So he didn't care about the farm?"

"He cared about owning it, but he didn't care about running it. He also cared about being a horse owner. He liked being at Saratoga and giving the jockeys advice as they mounted up and he loved being in the winner's circle, but he had far less interest in the work it took to get there."

"Tell me about this life insurance policy." We had reached the oak tree by now. It was a giant thing, rising high above the shed rows. It was cranking all of its energy into making new leaves and I could almost hear it hum. Brenda Stanley leaned against the trunk and flapped her eyelashes at me. She had high cheekbones and tidy little ears. I thought she looked

good enough to eat. Too bad she wasn't older and softer.
Old acorns kept crunching under my feet.

"There's not much to tell. Bernard showed it to me about
a month ago. I was surprised because he had become increasingly angry about Randall. He told me that he wanted me to
pretend that I had initiated the policy so that his son and
stepson wouldn't be jealous. I didn't think much about it at
the time."

"Were you surprised at the amount? Three hundred
thousand?"

"Not particularly. It wasn't as if I was expecting to see
the money anytime soon."

This could be true or false, but if it was false, then she
was a pretty good liar. She stared at me as if eager to know
what I would say next. "What's the name of the insurance
company?" I asked.

"I don't remember. I've got the policy on my desk in the
house. Do you want to see it now?"

"Later. How did Bernard feel about your getting twenty-
five percent of the farm at the time of his death?"

"I think he deeply regretted that prenuptial agreement
almost as soon as he made it. He asked me many times to
let him change it."

"And what did you say?"

She gave her blond hair a little toss. "I told him that a
girl had to look out for her future."

"What do you think he wanted?"

"He wanted to hold the whole of the farm himself. He
tried to buy Donald out as well, but Donald wouldn't even
talk about it. Anyway, Donald had no interest in doing anything that Bernard wanted."

"Do you think that Logan wanted to leave the whole
thing to Carl?"

"Possibly. I know that Bernard loved his son as much as

he was capable of loving anyone. Most likely he loved Carl because Carl hadn't done anything against him. Carl hadn't done anything wrong yet." The sarcasm in her voice was as obvious as a stick of butter smeared across a fingernail.

"What d'you think of Carl?"

"He's a boy. I don't have much use for boys. Oh, he's nice and pleasant and earnest, but I prefer men."

"Like Brickbrain?"

"Do you have to?"

"Sorry. Sometimes it just sweeps over me. What about McClintock?"

"He's a jerk. He sees himself as Carl's guardian angel, so he is always rushing around making sure that Carl's interests are being protected. He steps on a lot of toes."

I could see McClintock over toward the shed row. He had on a red jacket and was talking to Randall Hanks. Their body language was all angular and moody: lots of elbows and jerking motions. It didn't look like McClintock was asking Hanks to tango. Both seemed full of accusations.

"If Logan was murdered and you didn't do it," I asked, "then who do you suspect?"

Brenda looked me straight in the eyes. "I'd rather not say."

"Could Brickbrain do it by himself?"

"Of course not."

"Carl?"

"No, he wouldn't kill his father." She spoke of the death of her husband without a trace of grief. Even if she hadn't killed him, she certainly saw his death as convenient. I wouldn't say she was as hard as nails, but if she had a heart, then it was made out of the same stuff they make highways out of.

"You're shortening my list of suspects. What's this horse like, this Triclops?"

"He's a show horse. I've had him for years, even before we were married. Right now he's quite upset. I have no idea what got into him. He's always very calm."

"Let's go see him. I like looking a killer in the face."

"Triclops?"

"That's right. Maybe I'll ask him a few questions and he'll spill the beans."

She looked at me uncertainly. Some people just can't tell when I'm serious. "He's over in the hay barn away from the other horses," she said. "We thought that might help."

We began to walk along the fence. There was pasture on the other side and some old horses were munching the new grass. The chubby guy named Paul was nailing a slat to one of the fence posts. Brenda called to him.

"Could you give us a hand? We want to see Triclops."

Paul looked like he was being asked to open up the cage for King Kong, but he put down his hammer and followed along behind us. I could hear him muttering to himself. Brenda glanced at me and rolled her eyes. She was the kind of woman who liked to make inclusive/exclusive gestures. It was a way of separating people from one another, like cutting a horse out of a herd. It showed that she liked you but didn't like somebody else.

"What d'you think would have happened if Logan hadn't been killed?" I asked. "What were your plans?"

"Randall and I were going to leave. Being here just wasn't worth it anymore."

"That sounds cozy. What was going to happen to your part of the farm?"

"I owned nothing, I only stood to inherit that twenty-five percent. Donald wanted it. For all we knew, Bernard could have lived for twenty more years. Donald was willing to pay me a lot of money for it."

"How much?"

"Two hundred thousand."

"And now?"

"We haven't talked."

The barn was a big red thing with a hip roof and hay doors up at the top. Paul slid open the great door. He was a grumpy guy with a face like a blown-up paper bag, the sort of guy who would eat something every time he didn't get his own way. Ah, the solace of food. It looked like Paul didn't get his own way a lot. The proof of past frustrations was pushing at his belt.

There was a feed passage down the center of the barn and a big box stall at the end. The barn had a wooden floor and I could hear the clump clump of some big animal—presumably Triclops—from the stall. It was a nervous, dissatisfied banging which indicated that Triclops wasn't a happy camper.

Brenda opened the top half of the door of the stall and immediately Triclops shoved his head out. He was a big brown horse with a white splotch on his forehead. It was clear he recognized her and was happy to see her, but his eyes kept rolling around and he kept tossing his head. He looked like a creature that had had a nasty experience he was trying to forget. Maybe Freud could have helped him. Certainly it would take more than a carrot. Brenda opened the bottom half of the door.

"I wouldn't do that, ma'am," said Paul unhappily. "He tried to kick me yesterday."

"You had it lucky compared to Logan," I said.

Triclops wore a halter and Brenda Stanley took hold of the cheek strap and led him out into the feed passage. She was taking a chance, since Triclops had kicked someone to death less than twenty-four hours earlier. But she was a strange woman and this act of recklessness was part of it. She liked the fact that Paul was scared half to death and that

I had my back pressed to the wall hard enough to feel the splinters. Paul and I were not big brawny guys but we were still men and Brenda was showing us she could do something that we didn't have the guts to do. Triclops kept raising his knees higher than made sense and kept snorting. I checked his three white stockings for traces of Logan's blood, looking more for sensationalism than proof. They were clean but that didn't mean anything.

"See," she said, "he's perfectly safe."

At that moment a gray rat ran across the floor in front of her. Now, I've heard that elephants are supposed to be afraid of mice but no elephant could have been as terrified as Triclops at the sight of that rat. The horse screamed in a way I have never heard from an animal. He didn't seem to rear up so much as take all four feet off the floor. He levitated himself in a most violent manner. Brenda tried to hang on but she didn't have a chance. She was lifted up as well and flung aside. Triclops dashed at Paul, rearing up and still screaming. Paul looked as if no ham sandwich or bag of jelly doughnuts would ever comfort him again. His time appeared to be up. As for me, I popped back into Triclops's stall and shut the door. Whatever was going to happen, I didn't want to see it. The empty stall seemed the one safe place. I slammed the door. Then Paul started yelling.

When I opened the top door a few seconds later, Triclops was disappearing out of the barn, kicking up his white stockings and flying along. Brenda Stanley was sitting on the floor of the feeding passage with straw in her hair and looking stunned. Paul was rolling around on the floorboards gripping his arm. He had nothing of the brave little Spartan boy in him and he was yelping like a puppy.

As for the rat, it was nowhere to be seen.

5

I was just skulking out of the box stall when a little guy came tearing into the barn all ready to rip off somebody's head. Maybe he was in his forties, maybe he was fifty, whatever he was, he could sure run fast. In his left hand he was holding a bottle of Budweiser with his thumb over the top so it wouldn't spill.

"Who the hell let that horse get out? Don't you know he's dangerous?"

When he saw us, he face assumed an ah-I-thought-so sort of expression. He was the man I had seen with the stepson, Donald Croteau, earlier that morning leaning against the rail of the training track, but I hadn't paid much attention to him then. He was about five foot seven and wiry with old-fashioned long gray hair, like the style of a rock-and-roll bozo from around 1960: wings on the sides and a duck's ass in back. All he needed was a gray guitar to go with his gray hair. Maybe a little gray suit. He had ex-jock written all over him and he was even bowlegged. He stood looking at us like he wanted to separate our heads from our bodies. His beer bottle dangled from a couple of fingers. Although Paul was still moaning and holding his arm, the guy gave him all the sympathy that a robin gives a worm.

Brenda had gotten to her feet and was trying to stare the

guy down, but it seemed she had met her match. There wasn't
a lot of love in her expression. No sex on a hay bale for this
fellow, I thought.

"Did you do that, Miss Stanley?" asked the guy. "What
a stupid thing. Now I'll have to send ten men to catch him."

"I'll catch him myself," said Brenda, and she marched
out of the barn, leaving me with the ex-jock and the moaner.

"Hi," I said, "I'm Vic Plotz. Sorry about the horse, he
had an important appointment."

The ex-jock ignored me and went over to Paul. He wasn't
too gentle with him, prodding and poking his arm, and Paul
began to yelp. He yelped but he didn't complain, which made
me think the ex-jock inspired a certain nervousness among
the help. His gray rock-and-roll hairdo stayed as stationary
as a helmet.

"Jesus, she got your arm broke," he said. "Too bad the
horse couldn't have stomped her ass as well. I'll get someone
to drive you in to the hospital."

By now I was leaning over his shoulder watching Paul
grit his teeth. The ex-jock gave me an unfriendly look.

"Hi," I said again, "I'm Vic Plotz. I don't think we've
been formally introduced."

The fellow remained unmoved by my charm. "I don't give
a fuck who you are, but if you don't get off this property, I'll
turn you into dog meat." He had a little gray growl to go
with his gray haircut.

"No can do," I said cheerfully. "I'm gainfully employed."

"He's a kind of private detective from Saratoga," said
Paul, trying to be helpful.

"Not 'kind of,' young man," I said. "I'm a full-blooded
private detective."

"All right, wise guy," said the ex-jock. He made a grab
for me but I stepped back and he grabbed a handful of air.

He was just one more fellow trying to wrinkle my lapels, the third that day and it wasn't even lunchtime. It looked like I needed to change my tailor.

I tried one of my cordial smiles. "If you so much as lay a finger on me," I said, "I'll have you tied up in civil court for the next ten years. Compared to me Genghis Khan was like Snow White. Who do I have the pleasure of addressing?"

"Frankie Faber."

"Ah, the famous trainer. I should have known I was in the presence of an artist. Did you just come up from Belmont?"

"Last night. You got an employer? What's your right to be here?"

"Carl Logan hired me."

Frankie Faber took a sip of his beer. It seemed to console him. "Why?" he asked.

"Because his father thought someone wanted to kill him."

"You shittin me?"

So I explained how Bernard Logan had come into Charlie's office on Friday and how he believed that someone at the farm wanted to murder him, but I didn't say he had pointed his finger at his wife and Randall Hanks. Through all this Paul with the broken arm listened as closely as if I were giving directions on how to find the Holy Grail.

"Then when we got out here on Saturday morning," I said, "Logan was in the process of getting trampled to death."

"It's the rats, boss," said Paul. "Triclops is terrified of rats. And they're all over the place. I've never seen so many." He was standing up now and holding his arm as gently as a mother holds her baby.

"I know nothing about any of this," said Faber. "I've been down at Belmont all week." Then he shut his mouth so firmly that I could hear the click. It looked like silence was going to be his motto. I was struck, however, that he found nothing surprising in the possibility that Logan had been murdered.

"So you have no suspects?" I asked.

"I know nothing at all. Look, I gotta get this man to a doctor. Maybe I'll see you later, okay?"

He led Paul out of the barn, hurrying him along, and I followed. Faber hadn't seemed worried about Paul until I began making a nuisance of myself. I also remembered how Faber had looked at Brenda Stanley. There hadn't been any love lost on his side either, like he had despised her. And I wondered if Faber would have been so silent had he known that she and Hanks were the ones that Bernard Logan had accused, which made me wonder if Faber had another suspect in mind, which made me further wonder if he was afraid of anything, which made me further wonder if wondering was ever going to get me anyplace. The farm had too many bosses, too many people bossing other people around. Brenda Stanley and Hanks gave people orders, Croteau and Frankie Faber gave people orders, old man Logan had given people orders, even young Carl Logan and McClintock gave people orders. It was like all those cooks that screw up the soup. Everybody had a nickel's worth of power.

Outside, I blinked my eyes several times in the brightness of the morning. Over by the shed row, I could see Brenda hurriedly saddling a horse. Several stable hands were saddling up as well, including the kid I had hired to catch me some rats. I hoped he wasn't going slack on the job and forgetting our deal. I looked out across the fields for some sign of Triclops but there was none. He was probably galloping his heart out across the battlefield, trampling down the grass on all those places where Gentleman Johnny Burgoyne got his pride shaved to a nubbin.

It seemed strange that Triclops would have such a terror of rats. I mean, I don't expect any horse to chummy up to them—after all there's a basic size difference—but you'd think that horses would get used to having them around. There must have been lots of rats moseying through the barns and shed rows in the still watches of the night. Triclops wasn't a young horse. How could he have reached the mature age of ten if every time he saw a rat he went bonkers? Faber was leading Paul over toward the parking lot. I trailed along behind them, kicking a stone and wondering upon whom I should now inflict my professional acumen. Then I got an idea and turned off toward the shed row.

Just as I reached the corner of the building, Brenda came tearing by on a big black horse. I waved but she apparently had decided to put our friendship on the back burner. No smiles, no waves, no blown kisses. Three other guys galloped after her. It was a mystery to me why none of them fell off their horses. Maybe they put Velcro on their saddles. When my son was a kid, me and my wife once rented some horses when we went for a little vacation in the Catskills: two hours up a mountain and down. The torture to my ass was like a punishment for my dirty thoughts. I had welts the size of doubloons. Thirty-five years ago and that was the last time I have been on a horse. I saw no reason to do it again ever. I mean, what do they make cars for, right? I've already made my transportation choice.

I found the old guy in the denim suit and fat mustache who I had talked to on Saturday shoveling horse poop out of one of the stalls.

"Hey," I said, "long time no see."

He glanced at me, then went back to his horse poop.

"What's your name?" I asked him.

"Louie," he answered without looking up.

"I once had an aunt from St. Louie," I said. "The candy she made was quite gooey. I got a professional question for you."

Louie waited. Like if he saved his words like a miser saves his coins, he must have had an encyclopediaful by this time. He kept shoveling and I formulated my question.

"Are there always so many rats around here?" I asked.

Well, in my own modest way, I must have loosed a little dam, because Louie responded warmly.

"Fuckin rats, the place is crawling with them. I never seen so many fuckin rats. It's one of the plagues, right? Like one of the plagues in the Bible? In Egypt or someplace? Didn't they have a whole plague of fuckin rats? Rats in the bedroom, rats in the wall. Maybe it's like that, you know? Maybe it's connected to the millennium or something. I mean, you can't hit the year two thousand without weird shit beginning to happen. Like a car, right? You get a car up to a hundred thousand miles and it starts acting funny. The wheels shimmy, the fenders rattle. Stands to reason, right? The millennium's like that. The world's wearing out. They talk about it on cable, all those preachers, and these rats are the first concrete evidence that we're in for some very deep shit. I mean, we still got a few years to go. If the rats is this bad in 1993, then we're going to be up to our fuckin earlobes in rats when the millennium rolls around. You know what I've been thinking all morning? Invest in cats. That's going to be the big mo-neymaker. People will be buying cats hands over fist. Didn't those Egyptians worship cats? Can't blame them, can you? Kitty chow, catnip, the whole shebang—those stocks are going to go right through the ceiling. You got a cat? Breed him, get him laid, it's money in the bank."

Louie stood there breathless for a moment with his eyes whanging away in his head, then he went back to shoveling horse poop. It occurred to me that if you're shoveling horse poop at the age of sixty-five, then it is because a lot of other career choices were closed to you early on perhaps because of certain disadvantages in your makeup, and I wondered if Louie wasn't one of the mentally challenged, meaning crippled. I considered asking if the farm didn't have any cats, but I wasn't sure that my system could withstand the emotional shock of his answer.

"I'll take that under consideration," I told him, and I backed out of the stall. Actually I'd seen some cats, depressed-looking creatures, overwhelmed by the size of the task that lay before them, moping under a tree. But it seemed to me that if Battlefield Farms was suddenly plagued by rats, the reason for it was something other than millennial or even supernatural.

I was wandering along the shed row wondering who I could ask about this rat problem when I heard shouting. Since I was thinking about rats, I figured a bunch more had suddenly turned up, but that was just bad thinking because this had nothing to do with rats, or not directly.

Neil McClintock came flying backward out of Hanks's office at the end of the shed row and landed smack on his bottom in the dirt. As McClintock scrambled to his feet, Hanks came barreling out of the door and took a swing at him, missed and spun around. McClintock gave him a shove, then took a swing himself, batting at Hanks's ear.

McClintock had on a red jacket to match his red face and he had blood on his beard, presumably his own unless he had been nibbling steak tartar on the sly. Hanks took another swing at McClintock and missed, then McClintock grabbed him around the middle and they staggered back toward the door to the office. Both were cursing and accusing one another and I heard Logan's name being bandied about.

Other people started showing up from the stalls, grooms, stable hands and suchlike, but no one tried to interfere.

Hanks's pressed Levi suit was getting wrinkled and his starched black hair had loose pieces poking out in various directions. He gave McClintock a shove, then drew back and smacked him in the kisser. McClintock staggered away, wiping his mouth, then turned and tackled Hanks, so they both crashed to the ground. They rolled around in the mud and dirt, holding each other with one hand and trying to get in a few good hits with the other. These were not young guys. Both were over forty and I was impressed by their physical ability. I mean, when I want to hit somebody, I just take him to court. Isn't that what the courts are for? They allow us to beat up economically on those people whom we can no longer beat up physically.

Frankie Faber came running across the yard and young Carl Logan wasn't far behind him. Faber was a lot smaller than either of the two guys rolling and bellowing in the dirt, but he was a decisive cuss and he plunged right in without even saying a prayer or two, grabbing Hanks's collar and dragging him away. McClintock took the opportunity to get in two last licks and then Carl grabbed him as well.

"What the hell's going on here?" shouted Faber. "The whole fuckin place is falling apart!"

Hanks was standing back against the wall, rubbing his face as if checking to see if any pieces had been stolen. "Tell him to keep his accusations to himself!" he said.

McClintock shook himself free of Logan. "I know what you and that tart did!"

Before he could say more, Hanks rushed him and immediately the two men were rolling on the ground again, shouting and kicking. Faber dove back into the jumble of arms and legs. This time he invited a couple of the stable hands to go with him and they dragged Hanks away and back into his office as if they were used to heaving around hysterical galoots. Hanks could fight a little better than he could think, but he wasn't going to receive high marks in that field of activity either.

Young Carl Logan had his arm around McClintock and was leading him away. McClintock was angry and talking rapidly. Logan was soothing him. I couldn't hear what was being said because several stable hands were grumbling, wondering what the fuss was about. The stable hands looked anxious, and I saw Louie, the old guy who had told me about the rats, chewing his mustache and muttering to himself.

"All this must be very enlightening for you," said a voice behind me.

I turned to see Donald Croteau, standing with his hands in the hip pockets of his jeans. His ten-gallon hat was tilted back on his head and he bore a thoughtful expression.

"I didn't realize that horse work could be so much fun," I said. "Are these guys always like that?"

"Not recently."

"What d'you think happened?"

"I think someone made them start accusing each other."

"And who might that be?"

"You."

I scratched my head, then looked at my fingernail. "As a lady told me earlier today, you're mixing up the cause with the effect. I'm just a simple workingman."

"You're here to make people think that Logan was murdered."

"And wasn't he?"

"He was trampled by a horse, that's all I know. Who's hired you?" Croteau was one of those lipless wonder kind of guys, like two rubber bands stretched tightly together could make more of a pucker.

"Carl Logan."

"Why'd he do that?"

"Because his father thought someone wanted to kill him."

"Tell me about it."

So again I told the story of Bernard Logan showing up on Friday afternoon. I had mentioned it to Croteau on Saturday but this morning I gave him the complete version. I should have had the story printed on a card so I could pass it out to interested parties. It would have saved me lung power. But that wouldn't really have worked, because I changed the story a little for Croteau's benefit. I didn't tell him that Logan had suspected his wife and Randall Hanks. I made him think it was something to do with the farm.

"What kind of thing wrong with the farm?" Croteau had stopped being laid-back and casual. He was one of those people who seems as sleepy as day-old spaghetti until he loses his temper. He had a smooth face like Roy Rogers used to have: a smooth sunburnt oval with very fine wrinkles, blond eyebrows and light brown hair. He was a handsome parcel of goods but there was something mechanical about him, as if he had no emotional life or no feelings but anger.

"He said there was something funny going on with the horses, no more than that."

Croteau made a kind of smile that narrowed his eyes to slits. There wasn't any humor in it, he was just exercising his face. "Maybe we need to go someplace and talk," he said.

"Glad to."

"My house is over past the big one. I'll give you a cup of coffee."

It did my heart good to see how people warmed up to me once I had stated my business. Croteau and the others had buckets of secrets and I was right there to have them splashed across the bonfire of my curiosity. We strolled off toward his ranch house, and Croteau pointed out some promising two-year-olds on the other side of the fence.

Croteau's house seemed untouched by human hands. If it took a heap of living to make a house a home, then Croteau's place still had a Himalaya to go. There were no pictures, no books, no magazines or newspapers, no stereo equipment, no clothes lying around, no evidence of human habitation. The furniture could have been bought from any motel that was going bankrupt.

"You lived here long?" I asked.

"Twelve years. I had it built shortly after I came back from college and took over my part of the farm." Croteau removed his hat and set it carefully on the coffee table. It became the only ornament in the room.

"What do you do for fun?"

"What d'you mean?"

"It looks like you haven't moved in yet."

Croteau looked around, surprised that anybody might be critical of his living conditions. "I keep the TV in the bedroom," he said.

"That explains it," I told him.

The kitchen was as neat as the living room. No dirty dishes, no loaves of bread, no homey smell of freshly baked cookies. Croteau put a kettle on the stove, then took a jar of instant coffee out of the cabinet. When the cabinet door was opened, I saw that it contained nothing but the coffee and an unopened box of Ritz crackers.

"I hope you don't take milk or cream."

"I already decided against it. What about sugar?"

"I might have some somewhere."

"Don't worry. Have you thought of getting a pet?"

"They're dirty."

"What about a goldfish?"

Croteau gave me a look to indicate he knew I was joking but he didn't get the humor. He was wrong, I was perfectly serious. He needed an animal pal.

"What d'you think about all these rats that have been turning up?" I asked.

"I haven't seen any myself, although I heard some of the men talking about it."

"Just what do you do at the farm?" I asked. I figured Croteau had all the qualifications of a good lawn jockey. He could stand in the front yard with a little ring in his hand and people could tie horses to him. On the other hand, he liked to go out around dawn and run his Porsche at one hundred and twenty miles per hour on narrow roads. I guessed there was something in his makeup that I wasn't seeing.

"Most of my time is spent with Faber working with the horses. Often I'm at the track, which is Belmont right now. I also take horses out of state: Delaware, Maryland, Florida, once or twice to California. Faber takes care of the actual training, with my advice, and I take care of the business end of things. We breed a lot of horses and we stable a lot of mares from other farms."

"How long have you worked with Faber?"

"He's been here five years."

"You like him?"

"We work well together. He's efficient and knows his job."

"Sounds like a pal," I said.

The kettle gave a little shriek and Croteau poured the boiling water into my cup. He wasn't having any himself. "What did my stepfather mean that something funny was going on with the horses?" he asked.

I held the coffee cup, which was a blue mug with the word "Belmont" in white letters, and blew at the steaming surface.

"He said something about losing three good horses in claiming races, horses that shouldn't have been running in those races in the first place."

"Jesus Christ!" said Croteau, flaring up. "He was always

interfering." He calmed down again. His anger was like a sailor husband—it came and went.

"It was his farm."

"Forty percent of it's mine."

"So you can make forty percent of the fuckups?"

Croteau's tight face got a little tighter. "I don't know how much you understand about claiming races, Mr. Plotz, but there's always a risk. Logan had lost horses, everybody loses horses, just as everybody also claims horses. In the past two months we've had an unlucky streak, that's all."

"He said those horses should never have run in those races in the first place."

"He could have looked out for it. He could have been in charge. If he had a complaint all he needed to do was speak up. Instead he spent all his time in that greenhouse. Those horses we lost, we knew they had potential, that's all. Nobody was cheating anybody else. It was a simple error in judgment."

"Which happened three times."

Croteau looked as if he regretted giving me the cup of coffee. But it was too late to take it back: I had already burned my lips on it.

"Logan felt that somebody wanted to kill him," I said. "He wasn't sure of the reason. Maybe it had to do with the fact that his wife was having an affair with Randall Hanks. Maybe he felt something crooked was going on with the claiming races. Maybe it was something else. What did you think of Logan?"

Croteau studied my face, as if balancing whether to tell the truth or fib. "I hated him," he said at last.

"How come?"

"He was cold and unfeeling. He was selfish. He was vicious. Sometimes I even thought he was evil."

"Yeah, but what had he done recently?"

"Pardon me?"

"Forget it. What specific thing had he done? There must be something you can point to." We were still standing in the kitchen. Four yellow chairs were pushed up against a yellow Formica table but Croteau made no attempt to sit down and neither did I. The furniture had an unused and lonely look.

"My mother died of cancer fifteen years ago," said Croteau. "While she was dying, Logan completely ignored her. He was seeing other women. He even brought them to the house. She'd be lying in her bed and hear him and the women laughing. She'd even hear them fucking. Then when she was finally taken to the hospital, he refused to visit her. It was as if she never existed. I was surprised he even went to the funeral. But even the funeral he saw as an occasion to see old friends. He picked up a woman there, picked up a woman at his own wife's funeral."

Croteau let his sentence hang in the air and shimmer, as if it was something we could both stare at and feel shocked by. Talking, Croteau's voice had become hushed as if he could hardly believe the truth of his own words.

"So you decided to move back here and be pals?" I asked.

"I decided to move back here so that he would never be able to forget what he had done."

"Would you have killed him?"

"That would have let him off the hook too easily."

"You're a vindictive kind of guy," I said. "How could you train his horses, take care of his farm?"

"Forty percent of it was mine. It had belonged to my mother. It was something I was doing for her. Besides, I didn't want him to get his hands on it."

"And what do you think of Carl?"

"I wish he'd never been born."

"Other than that, what do you think?"

Logan made a little snapping gesture with his teeth, as if swallowing a tidbit of anger. I guessed he would never appreciate my sense of humor. He was just one more person I wouldn't be inviting to my birthday party.

"I have little to do with him. I neither hate him nor love him. He hardly exists for me. Actually, until last summer I almost never saw him. He was away at college, then at boarding school before that. He moved back here after he graduated."

"Just like you," I said.

"Just like me."

"You think that he too had a grudge against his father?"

"I know nothing about it. I hardly ever speak to him."

"But he has horses. He works with McClintock. The horses all run under the same colors: Battlefield Farms."

"That's going to change," said Croteau, speaking with a kind of violent precision. "With my stepfather dead, I'm the major stockholder. McClintock is out of here. Even Randall Hanks is out of here. Once the will is cleared, they'll be gone and I'll be making the decisions."

"What if Carl and Brenda join forces?" I suggested. "They hold sixty percent of the farm between them."

It seemed this idea hadn't occurred to Croteau. He considered it. "They've got no use for one another. You saw what happened just now between McClintock and Hanks."

"But they might be willing to make a deal in order to cut you out. Business conquers all, right?"

I could see that these were unhappy thoughts for Donald Croteau. "We'll see," he said after a moment.

I tried to imagine the place run by three people who hated each other: the shifting allegiances and animosities. It sounded like heart trouble at an early age. I felt sorry for young Logan. He at least seemed like a good Joe, but I could have been wrong about that as well.

"What about Brenda?" I asked. "What's your take on her?"

Croteau shrugged. "She's a whore. She thinks with her pussy. Recently she's been making my stepfather miserable. I've been grateful for that. Otherwise, we have nothing to do with one another. I mean, she's hardly human. She's driven by her animal desires."

"And what are you driven by?"

"My will, my reason, my revenge."

"I hear you like to drive your car fast at daybreak," I said.

Croteau's mouth lifted slightly at the corners. "My weakness," he said.

"What do you like about the Porsche?"

"It has as a machine all the qualities which I aspire to as a human being."

I wondered if Croteau saw himself as a shining example of the human race: Boy Scout leader and group therapy champ. I couldn't see that living at Battlefield Farms would be a picnic. I began to sympathize with Brenda Stanley and her tryst on the hay bale. No wonder it was called Battlefield Farms. They were lucky it wasn't called Slaughter Manor.

"Tell me again about these rats," I asked, swinging the subject into a sharp left turn. "How come there're so many?"

Croteau looked immediately bored with the subject. "Any farm has rats."

"They made Triclops absolutely hysterical. Wouldn't he be used to them?"

"What do you mean?"

So I told him how I had asked to see Triclops and how Brenda had brought him out of the stall in order to show off her muscle and then Mr. Rat had shown up in his little fur suit and Triclops went bonkers. "Why would he be like that?" I asked.

"I have absolutely no idea."

But Croteau had his eyes on me and I could see he was no longer bored by the subject. It was something inexplicable even to him. More than inexplicable, it was downright suspicious.

"Do you know if any dead rats were found in the stall with your stepfather?"

"No. I had to help catch that damn horse. Then, because of the death, I had a lot of phone calls to make. Are you saying there're more rats around here than usual?"

"Hey, it's your farm."

"I've been down at Belmont."

"Who would know about the rats?"

"Randall Hanks, presumably. He's in charge of the buildings and grounds."

"Maybe I'll go ask him," I said, setting down my coffee cup. I hadn't finished the instant java but I didn't think Croteau would be offended. His ego wasn't wrapped up in his cooking, only revenge. "If there were dead rats in that stall, it might say something about why Triclops went crazy."

"I think I'll come as well." Croteau retrieved his cowboy hat from the coffee table. There was a ridge around his light brown hair, like a string mark around his head, and the hat fitted comfortably into it.

• ● •

Randall Hanks's office was in the corner of one of the shed rows. Two stalls had been knocked together to make it, and the office had a horsey flavor. It was empty but the door was unlocked, which I took as an invitation. I went in and looked around. Donald Croteau followed me. Outside we

had seen Brenda Stanley and three stable hands leading Triclops across the yard. The poor horse had ropes all over him
and looked like one ragged creature: muddy and with leaves
and dead grass caught up in his mane and fetlocks. Triclops
was a textbook example of an anxiety crisis and he needed
only a horse-sized couch in order to lie back and tell his
troubles to the horse shrink. Or maybe they could mix Prozac
with his feed.

The office was a kind of boy's room: rugged and utili-
tarian. Bare wooden walls painted white and a rough wooden
floor painted black. There was a calendar on the wall from
some feed company with a reproduction of two horses galloping flirtatiously, but this was the only art. An old wooden
desk, some battered chairs, four file cabinets, several closets.
The only new thing was an IBM computer but there were
dirty fingerprints on the keyboard and smudges on the mon-
itor. I tried the belly drawer of the desk but it was locked.
Croteau stood by the door.

"What do you think of Hanks?" I asked.

"He does his job and services the boss's wife."

"Sounds like a happy life," I said.

The first closet was filled with stacks of papers, old form
books and racing programs from a dozen tracks. It had a
musty smell. A few dead flies lay on their backs on the floor,
poor things. The other closet had some rain gear, boots, some
old coats, nothing that had been worn for a while and the
boots had a layer of dust. I pushed the coats aside. Something
like a baseball bat was leaning against the wall in the corner.
I pulled it out. It was heavy and made of metal and wasn't
a baseball bat. It had some kind of battery thing at the handle
end and a place for a plug. The object looked like a wand
that an evil genie might use.

"What's this?" I asked.

"A cattle prod. Be careful, it might still have a charge."

It was at that moment that Hanks opened the door. Young Carl Logan was a few steps behind him.

"What're you doing in here?" asked Hanks. Then: "Where'd you get that thing?"

"I found it in the closet," I said.

"You're lying."

"Not today," I said. "Yesterday, maybe; the day before, why not? But not today."

"There wasn't any prod in there." Hanks was still a little rumpled from his fight with McClintock. He had dusted himself off and brushed his black hair but there were mud stains on his jeans. He looked unhappy and traces of suspicious thoughts moved across his brow like fat crows across a cloudy sky.

"That's where he found it," said Croteau. "What was it doing there, Randall?"

Hanks turned on Croteau. "If he got that prod from my closet, then you or somebody else put it there! What the hell's going on?"

"You're paranoid," said Croteau.

Hanks gave him a shove, knocking him into Carl Logan. Croteau's face bled white, then he dove at Hanks, hitting him hard and knocking him back across the desk. I jumped out of the way and a chair fell over. Carl started shouting at them to break it up, but they paid no attention. I never saw such a place for excitable people. How could they ever get any work done? It seemed that every single one of them was just waiting to take a swing at someone else.

The two men were wrestling on the floor. Croteau's cowboy hat had rolled away and Carl picked it up. Hanks was stronger than Croteau and was soon sitting astride him and punching his face as he shouted, "You put it there, you son of a bitch!"

There was a little switch at the bottom of the prod. I

flicked it on and felt the contraption hum. It was a cheery kind of feeling. I stretched it forward until the tip of the prod touched the seat of Randall Hanks's Levi's. Well, let me tell you, if you want to get a guy's immediate attention, I now know how to do it. I touched his rump and Hanks soared upward. He shouted and climbed the air, grasping at dust motes with his fingernails. He hooted like they say a banshee hoots. It was a wonderful display of frantic energy, and I couldn't imagine how I had gotten through my life without owning such a handy item.

6

Early that Monday evening I drove out to Charlie's place on the lake. There was still a lot of sunlight and some reckless yokels were racing their speedboats out on the water, sending up curtains of spray as they spun their boats in figure eights. From the road their boats sounded like petulant chainsaws. I had gotten home from Battlefield Farms around the middle of the afternoon and had spent an hour or so catching up on the stock market, pleased to see that it had continued its modest climb without me. Some of my stocks were up, some were down, but mostly they were thriving, which made me pat my palms together.

I had also driven over to the biker's place—meaning my duplex—just to see if it was still standing. I sat in my Mercedes for about five minutes and studied the fine lines of Ernie's Harley. Ernie Flako—what kind of name is that? It sounded like convict genes to me, the name of a serial killer. Ernie was nowhere in sight. Maybe he was inside getting stoned or exploring the jungle tattoos on Puma's breasts or playing Gnaw the Baby with his pit bull. Whatever he was doing, he didn't come out onto the stoop and wave. That didn't bother me none. Ernie Flako was no longer the affliction he had been earlier that day because I now had a plan.

A healthy stock market and a plan for Ernie Flako, I

should have been sitting on top of the world, but in the mail that afternoon I received a letter from my granddaughter, Susannah. Like now that she had decided to spend the summer with her grandpop, she wanted to write thirty-five times a week just to show how much she cared. She asked me about Sharri Tefila, the Jewish Community Center, and Temple Sinai. She asked me how well I knew the rabbi. She said their rabbi in Evanston was a close personal friend of the family and came to dinner once every two weeks. She asked if I could invite the rabbi at Temple Sinai to dinner as well. Of course we must already be close friends, she said. To tell the truth, I wouldn't know the rabbi of Temple Sinai if he came up and slapped me across the face with a pork chop. I wished him well. Like I say, I absolutely adore religious people, but I didn't intend to start trading lunch bags with him.

Then Susannah asked about what kind of youth groups they had at the temple and Bible study and Hebrew lessons. She asked about the Anti-Defamation League and about my own political involvement with Zionist causes. She spoke of youth groups in the Chicago area and how she wanted to memorize the Bible and could already recite the Book of Genesis and hoped to memorize Exodus soon. She promised to recite them to me when she came. She said these recitations were a great comfort to her and she hoped they would be a comfort to me as well. I tell you, I could hardly read her letter my hands were shaking so much. How was I going to live with this little girl? She had all the sense of humor of a flyswatter. I couldn't understand why she wanted to visit me. Why come to Saratoga Springs when she could go to Israel? Didn't she want to work on a nice kibbutz? It seemed her only purpose in coming was to make me go amok. I would have to keep my mouth shut, take the nude pictures off the walls, internalize my farts and probably get my cat, Moshe

III, circumcised. It was enough to make me become a Buddhist.

So these were the issues which were on my mind as I drove around the lake to Charlie's place. Logan, schmogan, I had real problems. What was death compared to these? I realized the truth of the remark that gray hairs were the child's gift to its luckless parents. At first I had wondered why Matt and his wife were letting their twelve-year-old daughter come to Saratoga. Now I realized they must be urging her to go. Probably they were driving her from the house with a stick. No more recitations of the Book of Genesis for them. They planned to put their feet up and have an easy summer.

I found Charlie sitting at the end of his dock reading a book about the old Loomis Gang in upstate New York. He tried to tell me about it. "They stole horses," he said.

"Look," I said, "their problems were nothing to my problems. Anyway, they're lucky. They died a long time ago. They probably didn't even know their grandchildren."

"You want a Budweiser?"

"Jack Daniel's, if you please."

I followed him into the house. Charlie wore his old blue seersucker suit that smelled of mothballs. His hair was sticking up in peaks and he wore these dirty bucks with tar spots on their red soles. There were thumbprints on the lenses of his bifocals. As a fashion statement he was equivalent to a car wreck.

"So how was jury duty?" I asked.

He turned on me with a touch of venom. "I sat in the room the whole day! They never even got to me."

"Were you dismissed?"

"No, I've got to go back tomorrow."

"Did you get to hear any interesting cases?"

"This guy might have broken into this Sunoco station or

he might not have broken into the Sunoco station. There was a lot to be said on both sides. At the end of it I was willing to buy him the Sunoco station! Tomorrow I'll take my Walkman and a deck of cards."

"Take a cattle prod, they're all the rage."

He handed me a Jack Daniel's with a couple of ice cubes, then made one for himself. "You hungry?" he asked. "I could put some hamburgers on the grill."

"Sure," I said. "Splurge."

"What did you learn out at Logan's?"

"That place is full of people who hate each other," I said. "I've never seen so much tension. Maybe it's the rats, maybe rats make people nervous like that. Like we could sell tickets to graduate psych students so they could study stress at the source. It's a living psychology experiment."

"Tell me about it," Charlie said.

So I talked as Charlie dug the charcoal grill out of his shed, then cleaned it off with steel wool because he hadn't used it since the previous summer, then he dumped in the charcoal and starter and lit it, singeing his eyebrows. As the charcoal burned, he made four hamburger patties in the kitchen. I told him about the horse going bonkers, my conversations with Brenda Stanley and Donald Croteau, the fights between Hanks and McClintock and Hanks and Croteau, and of course the rats. Charlie made a salad with lettuce, tomatoes and cucumbers, then dumped a can of Boston baked beans into a pan and put it on the stove. He doesn't have a microwave. By the time the fire was ready, I'd finished my story and was on my second Jack Daniel's.

"Jesus, Victor, you have all the luck. Why buy a cattle prod when you can have fun like that?"

"That's not the half of it," I said. So I told him about Ernie Flako and the letter from my granddaughter, and how both Ernie and Susannah were trying to shorten my life by making me worry too much and brood about inconsequentials.

"That's quite a gift," said Charlie as he put the burgers on the grill, "being able to recite Genesis. You should be proud." This was Charlie's idea of humor. Rudimentary, right?

"I'll bring her over and we can hear it together."

"Your bottle of Jack Daniel's or mine?"

"Yours, most likely," I said. "Susannah said she hopes I don't drink or smoke. I almost started smoking again just to spite her."

"She'll make a religious man of you," said Charlie. "It's probably not too late to become a rabbi yourself. It'll be something to keep you busy in your later years."

When I first met Charlie Bradshaw nearly twenty years ago, he had no sense of humor. A few limericks, a few traveling-salesman jokes, but that was it. Over the long haul, I've worked with him, helping him nurse his little nubbin along until he can almost tell a story that will elicit a faint chuckle. And what does he do? He aims this firehose of fancy at me and throws the switch. Power corrupts, there's no doubt about it.

"Did you get an autopsy report on Logan?" I asked.

"I called just before you got here. They certainly did nothing like a complete autopsy, but there was one blow from the horse's hoof that could have killed him and there was evidence he'd had a heart attack as well. One can hardly blame him. The state investigators are listing it as an accidental death. What d'you think of this business with the rats?"

By now the hamburgers were done and we were sitting at a small picnic table by the water. It was cool and we'd have to go in soon, but the sun was just setting across the lake and it made the water go all pink. I was on my third

Jack Daniel's and was slowly getting smoothed out, like a rumpled shirt during a good ironing. Charlie had put some cheddar cheese on the burgers and there were buns as well. Now and then a fish flopped out of the lake, but I was always too slow to see it.

"The rats seem a mystery to everybody. Hanks told me that two or three dead rats had been found in Triclops's stall along with Logan's body. I mean, it's not as if the place is crawling with rats, but, as Hanks said, they normally don't see many. They got cats and they also set out poison. And it's rats that scare the bejesus out of Triclops."

"What about this cattle prod?"

"That seems a mystery as well. Nobody has claimed it, nobody knows what it was doing in the back of Hanks's closet. Hanks himself said that somebody's trying to frame him, but when I asked who, he just clamped his square jaw shut and shook his head. He's got all the brains of a tree toad in heat. He goes duh, duh, dribbles his lip, and Brenda Stanley looks at him as if he'd been reciting 'The Shooting of Dan McGrew.' "

" 'A bunch of the boys were whooping it up in the Malamute Saloon,' " recited Charlie. " 'The kid that handles the music-box was hitting a ragtime tune . . .' "

"Don't you start now, Charlie. Genesis is bad enough."

"You know," said Charlie, "if a whole bunch of rats have suddenly shown up at Battlefield Farms, then somebody must have brought them there, which means that somebody must have bought them someplace. There can't be many places that sell gray rats."

"These looked like regular Norwegian rats," I said, being helpful. "I could tell by their accents."

"I think I'll ask Eddie Gillespie to do a little work for us. Maybe he can find out where the rats came from."

Gillespie is a guy in his early thirties who used to be a

car thief. Charlie helped him out when he was a cop, and actually Charlie has been helping him out ever since, getting him jobs and nudging him along. Eddie worked as a bartender in Charlie's mother's hotel and now he has some job with heavy equipment, fooling around with a backhoe. He got married a while back and he has a kid. The trouble with Eddie is that he has all the vanity of an overbred rooster. He's sassy, self-confident and sure that everything he does is brilliant. This might be all right if Eddie had a brain, but what he has in fact is a breadbox in his head. If you opened it up, you'd find a few crumbs, maybe a moldy bran muffin. That's what Eddie thinks with—that moldy bran muffin. He makes Randall Hanks look like a college president. The two of them should go on a dumbo quiz show and the first one to spell c-a-t would get a quarter for his parking meter. Charlie hires Eddie now and then for these little detective jobs and nearly every time something goes wrong.

"You think Eddie's the man for the job?" I asked.

"He could use the work."

"That doesn't answer my question. I don't think Eddie could find a rat if you sent him into the sewer with a semi-truck full of Swiss cheese."

"You're just envious because he's handsome," said Charlie.

"That's not handsome," I said. "A guy doesn't hit true handsome until he's over fifty. Eddie's like junket, like raspberry Jell-O. It's not stuff a real woman would go for."

By now we had finished the burgers and mopped up the salad and Boston baked beans. "Speaking of food," said Charlie, "I don't have any dessert unless you want to toast some marshmallows over the grill."

"I would but you'd tell on me later."

"Then let's go out to Battlefield Farms. I'd like to look around."

"What about the Queen of Softness?" I complained.

"The longer you wait," said Charlie, "the softer she'll be."

.   ●   .

We drove out Battlefield Road. It was dark by now and lights were burning in the few houses we passed. Away from the lake the air felt soft. I had the windows open and the top cranked back: a little square of light for a parachutist to come bopping through. Sometimes the warm air in spring can feel like velvet and such times always make me remember past springs and past happy occasions, so I would get little glimmers of my son when he was a kid and my wife when she was healthy. It seemed nice but maybe it wasn't nice. Maybe those velvet evenings were out there to trick you into lowering your guard. See how nice everything is? says the world. Then, when you lower your guard and take a peek, the world smacks you with a brick.

"So has your mother got the Bentley opened up yet?" I asked.

Charlie made a groaning noise. "It will open Memorial Day weekend. They've been painting and cleaning all month. She's got a string quartet lined up for opening day."

"That sounds like fun. Want me to hire a stripper?"

"Only if you can put her into a Victorian dress."

"You going to be working there this summer?" Charlie had once worked at the Bentley as hotel detective and once as night manager. Both occasions were very painful for him. He said that working for his mother made him revert in spirit to a petulant fourteen-year-old, meaning he overate, overcomplained and pouted. The hotel has become a landmark of Victorian antiques. There was once even talk about not accepting guests unless they promised to wear old-timey clothes and speak in complete sentences. A few years ago I worked as hotel detective as well and now I am about as popular at the Bentley as a black widow spider on a fudge brownie.

"I won't actually be at the hotel," said Charlie, "but I'm being retained as a consultant."

"Money for nothin, chicks for free," I said. "You can't beat it."

Charlie made a noise like a tire deflating. "That's not true. Eddie Gillespie will probably be head of security and I'll be advising him."

"Sounds like circus nights and thankless days," I said. "Now that *Dizzy* Gillespie has gone to his reward, Eddie's a prime candidate to inherit his name. Or maybe we could call him Giddy Gillespie. Or Flighty or Foggy or Groggy or Daffy. Maybe even Silly, maybe Wacky. It will look good on a business card: 'Goofy Gillespie: Solver of Crimes, almost.' "

"You don't like him because he's virile," said Charlie.

"Calling Goofy Gillespie virile is like calling a fence post smart. Anybody can stand up straight."

• ● •

Charlie had called Carl Logan before we left, and when I pulled the Mercedes into the parking lot by the greenhouse, young Logan and McClintock were waiting for us. We got out of the car and shook hands.

"Have any more fights today?" I asked.

"I don't know what's got into everybody," said Logan.

I gave a happy smile. "Murder," I said.

"I'd like to see the stall where your father was killed," said Charlie.

McClintock led the way. His salt-and-pepper beard and mustache seemed to shine in the dark. He was a big man and had a bearlike silhouette. "We've kept the stall empty. Haven't even cleaned it up except for getting rid of the dead rats. They would have smelled."

It was nearly nine o'clock and there was no one about. Lights were on in the big house and in Croteau's house as well. I imagined these people off nursing their resentments. The shed rows had big security lights at either end, and there was also a security light over the front door of the horse barn. Now and then I could hear a whinny or the clump of a hoof against a wooden floor. The air smelled of straw and manure.

"What's happened to Triclops?" I asked.

"He's been heavily sedated," Carl told me. "The vet was out here. He said that Triclops might have to be destroyed if he doesn't pull out of this."

"Did he make any suggestion about what had happened to the horse?" asked Charlie.

McClintock spat into the grass. "He made it pretty clear that he thought somebody had fucked with him. He didn't make any specific charges but he said a phobia like that wasn't natural. The poor horse was trembling all over."

Logan pulled back the door of the horse barn and flicked on a light. A rat scuttled across the floor ahead of us.

"There's another one!" said Logan. "I don't see where they're coming from."

McClintock led the way to the stall where old man Logan had been killed, opened the door and turned on another light. It was a dim bare bulb set into a porcelain fixture on the wooden ceiling, but Charlie had a big cop flashlight and he flashed it around the corners. Charlie loves cop paraphernalia and sometimes when he's had a couple of drinks he shows me his handcuffs and old billy club. Never his gun, though, he doesn't trust me with it.

Charlie poked around in the straw. I stood by the door. I had seen bloodstains and didn't want to get them on my shoes, even though they were dry by now. I have a squeamish streak and the sight of blood makes my knees feel funny. Carl Logan stood beside me with his hand in the hip pockets of his jeans and looked depressed. Charlie picked up some straw and studied it, then he picked up a piece of string. All he needed was a magnifying glass and a deerstalker hat and he'd be another Sherlock Holmes. I was going to say something like that but he looked too serious for jokes. Me, I don't have that problem. Life is never too serious for jokes. If you quit laughing, you might as well tuck yourself into the ground and say night-night. Charlie turned his light toward the ceiling. There were cracks in the boards with straw peeking through, then a small dark open space in the corner with more straw.

"What's up there?" asked Charlie.

Logan looked up at the ceiling. "Just a loft. There's some old tack stored up there. I don't know what else."

"Anyone been up there?" asked Charlie.

"Not that I know," said Logan.

"How do I reach it?"

"There's a ladder back by the rear door of the barn," said McClintock.

Charlie headed toward the door of the stall. "Coming, Victor?"

"I'll wait here and see what you find," I said. Those old lofts are treacherous. You're always putting your foot down on some seemingly solid place, then sinking through to your hip. The only action my bones like these days is sexual action.

Charlie clumped off with Logan and McClintock, leaving me by myself in the stall. It suddenly seemed a little dimmer, a little lonelier. I thought of old man Logan being killed just a few feet away and I didn't like it. A mean old fart like him was bound to produce an evil sort of ghost. Not that I believed in ghosts, of course, but there might be emanations or spiritual residues. And I bet they wouldn't be friendly. They'd get a kick out of scaring the bejesus out of me. I put my back to the wall and took deep breaths. A horse whinnied in another stall and I jumped. After a few minutes I heard feet clumping over my head and muttering voices. Now and then a glimmer of light flashed through one of the holes in the ceiling. When the footsteps got right over my head, they started moving faster, like they were doing a little dance. The muttering grew louder and more excited. I found myself thinking they had found money up there. Maybe jewels.

"What is it?" I called. "What did you find?"

Charlie made a noise that sounded like "Ahclaw!"

"What is it? I can't hear you!"

"A cage," shouted Charlie. "We found a cage!"

"What kind of cage?"

"A cage for rats!"

In a few minutes Charlie was back at the door of the stall. He looked like one happy sleuth with wisps of straw on his seersucker suit and his sparse hair standing up in peaks. He was holding a wire-mesh cage which measured about three feet by three feet by two feet. It had a door that was raised by a pulley and a piece of broken string was attached to it. Both Logan and McClintock had surprised looks on their faces: most likely impressed to be seeing detective science in action.

"It was right over that hole," said Charlie. "I bet the state police lab would find rat hairs all over it."

"To say nothing of fecal matter," I said. "How'd it work?"

"Simple," said Charlie. "Logan came into the stall and the murderer pulled the string opening this door, and all the rats tumbled down on top of Triclops."

"But why would that drive Triclops crazy?" I asked. "I

mean, why rats instead of something else, like birds or centipedes. Personally, I can't stand centipedes."

McClintock had taken the cage and was sliding the door
back and forth. The wire mesh was dark green.

"Because someone made Triclops scared of rats," said
Charlie. "That's where the cattle prod comes in. You show
Triclops a rat, then give him a shock. You show him another
rat and give him another shock. After a while, he's got a
phobia. There's an idea like that in an English mystery novel.
I bet you'd find a copy if you looked around."

"Why would Logan have come into the stall?" I asked.

"The murderer just probably lured him in. The string
could have been hanging just outside the door. Logan goes
in and the murderer shuts the door and pulls the string. Logan
gets stamped to death and a couple of rats get stamped as
well." Charlie flashed his light along the bottom of the walls.
"The other rats scramble out through these holes and cracks
and we've been seeing them ever since. I wonder who was
the first person who came along after Logan was killed?"

"I don't know," said young Logan quietly, "but we can
find out." He had his chin stuck out in a resolute way.

"Why didn't the murderer get rid of the cage?" I asked.

"I'm not sure," said Charlie. "I mean, nobody would have
even thought of murder if Logan hadn't talked to you on
Friday afternoon. It would have been seen as no more than
a nasty accident. Then maybe the murderer hasn't had the
time to get the cage, or planned to get it when nobody was
around. Maybe it's been too busy around here."

There was a noise at the front of the barn. Randall Hanks
entered carrying a flashlight as big as Charlie's. He stopped
when he saw us and his handsome face got that dull suspicious
expression again. He had changed into slacks and a soft gray
shirt. His hair was shiny and wet as if he had just come from

the shower, but maybe it was gel. Now that the boss was dead, he could hang out in the boss's house with the boss's wife anytime he wanted.

"What're you doin in here?" he asked. It was not a question motivated by friendly inquisitiveness.

"We're investigators, aren't we?" I asked. "We're investigating."

"Be quiet, Victor," said Charlie. Then, to Hanks, "What brings you over here?"

"I saw the lights and was curious. What's that cage?"

McClintock was so angry that he began to sputter through his beard. "It's where the rats came from. It was over Triclops's stall! Somebody dumped them on top of the horse so the horse would go crazy and kick Logan to death."

Hanks became very quiet. He didn't like what he was hearing and he wasn't sure what to make of it. "If there was any cage up there," he told McClintock angrily, "then you put it there."

"That's a lie!" said McClintock. He took a step toward Hanks, but Carl Logan and I grabbed his arms. I couldn't afford for there to be fighting when I didn't have my cattle prod. There wouldn't be any fun in it.

"Why would McClintock put the cage up there?" asked Charlie as mild as butter.

"Because he's trying to frame me. He thinks it's an easy way to get me outta here."

McClintock's muscles gave a little surge but Carl and I held on tight.

"Then who do you think killed Logan?" asked Charlie.

"The fuckin horse killed him, that's who."

"Perhaps," said Charlie, "but somebody made the horse do it. Somebody made Triclops terrified of rats, then dumped a bunch of rats on his head when Logan was in his stall.

That's what I'm asking you about. Triclops was no more than the weapon."

Hanks blinked a number of times, which I took to be external evidence of frantic thought. It seemed this idea of murder was as new to him as the sewing machine once was to Mr. Singer, but perhaps Hanks found lying simple. Perhaps the dumbo persona was just a front.

"McClintock's been hanging around here," said Hanks. "Why don't you ask him?"

"I will," said Charlie.

"The trouble is," said Carl, "everyone's in and out of here all day long."

"Motive and opportunity," I said, "that's what the detective business is all about."

"Somebody had to get the rat cage up into the loft early Saturday morning," said Charlie. "Where were you Friday night and Saturday morning, Mr. Hanks?"

Hanks chewed his upper lip for a moment, but he wore a dissatisfied look, as if his upper lip would never replace a T-bone steak. Then he said, "You got questions for me, you can ask them through my lawyer."

He backed out of the barn as if afraid that someone might shy a brick at him, then he disappeared.

"He had plenty of reasons to kill Logan," said McClintock, "beginning with Brenda Stanley."

"Would you like to have a family with Brenda Stanley on a hay bale," I poeticized, "or would you care to err with her on some other prickly substance?"

"Motive and opportunity," said Charlie. "Victor's right. Anybody could have done it."

$$\bullet \quad \bullet \quad \bullet$$

By eleven-thirty that night I was downtown at the Parting Glass chatting with Arnette Stroud from the *Saratogian*.

Charlie had asked me to find Eddie Gillespie to see if he wanted to do a little job for us. I had looked in half a dozen bars, but I hadn't found him, nor had he been at home. Eddie seemed to spend as little time at home as possible.

The Parting Glass is a big dark barn of a place on Lake Avenue about a block from the police station, with too much cigarette smoke and too much Guinness. Like it does Irish the way Tiffany's does jewels. Sometimes Irish bands show up and tweedle on their pipes. It's a hellish place to be on St. Patrick's Day.

Arnette Stroud has a regular column in the *Saratogian* where he comments on activities around town and tries to be as boring as possible. "The Cub Scouts of Pack 36 had a devilishly clever project last week," he might begin a column, "that involved empty beer cans and coat hangers." Before you even hit the end of the first sentence, you're yawning like crazy. Whenever I can't sleep at night, I read Arnette Stroud and within seconds I'm snoring like a baby.

Stroud didn't like me. Strangely enough, he felt I didn't take him seriously. He thought I teased him too much. Like any columnist, for even the worst paper, he believed that he had ten thousand readers who would kill to read his drivel. Stroud was a pear-shaped hunk of lard who kept his belt cinched tight above his belly, which made him look pregnant, like he was going to give birth to an old Remington typewriter. He was in his forties with muttonchop whiskers and curly brown hair sculpted by a local scissor man called Leonardo by his customers and Benny by his mom. The muttonchop whiskers existed to show people that Stroud was something special. The hairdo tried to argue that a smart head topping meant smart thoughts inside. Stroud was a person who felt he had already learned all the world had to teach and it was now his job to impart his knowledge. I could have insulted him all night long. We were both drinking Guinness. In fact, in my devious way, I had even bought the round.

"Tell me a little more about your involvement with witchcraft, Mr. Plotz," said Stroud.

"Call me Vic," I said, giving him a friendly poke in the belly with an index finger. "My experiments with witchcraft have been very promising. I've found that if I slaughter a black rooster under conditions which I'm not at liberty to divulge, I can make somebody I dislike fall down and break his leg."

"Astonishing," said Stroud. "And what else?"

"There are wonderful experiments with pentagrams and making oneself invisible. The master, of course, was Aleister Crowley, who was able to destroy rival magicians in psychic duels and said he had killed hundreds of babies in blood sacrifices at his estate in Sicily. I'd love to do something like that, but it's hard to get a baby around Saratoga. You think you could get me one, Mr. Stroud? You have important connections."

"Wouldn't it be wrong to kill a baby, Mr. Plotz?"

"I don't know. Aren't there an awful lot of babies? Maybe I could find a retarded one or a crippled one. What do you think? Would the Prince of Darkness mind if the kid had a harelip or was maybe missing a foot? Actually, better than a baby would be a teenage girl, maybe someone around twelve or thirteen. A virgin. There's always a short supply of those."

I talked like this for a while. Stroud looked like a fellow who had crawled through Death Valley on his belly and someone was now putting water onto his tongue drop by drop. I bought him another Guinness but he was so excited that he never touched it. After a while, I excused myself to go to the bathroom. When I came back, I saw that Stroud had his pad out and was writing as frantically as John Keats composing an ode. It did my heart good to see him so busy. In fact, he looked so happy that I couldn't bear to interrupt him. I went back to the phone to call the Queen of Softness. Was she interested in a nocturnal visit from a special friend? She said she would be delighted.

My car was parked around the corner. I drove out Route 29 toward Schuylerville to Rosemary's lunch counter, which is simply called Rosemary's: Family Eats Can't Be Beat. She has a little house behind it. I parked around back. The lights were out, which didn't bother me. Sometimes she plans little surprises for me. My feet made crunching noises across the cinders. I climbed the back steps, then let myself in with my key. The door led to the kitchen and the light on the stove said it was just midnight, the witching hour. I turned on the light in the hall.

"Rosemary," I called.

There was a noise from the bedroom, which was dark. It was the water bed sloshing and whooshing.

"Have you eaten?" called Rosemary in a sultry voice.

"I could use a snack."

"Come on in then."

I entered the bedroom and flicked the switch lighting a small lamp with a red shade on her night table. Rosemary lay in the middle of the water bed. She was naked, more or less. Years ago she must have had an hourglass figure. Now she had a figure like a rolled-up mattress. Her hair was platinum blond, even the pubic hair. It came from a bottle, of course. Rosemary's big breasts fell on either side of her, sliding toward her armpits. Her belly was all putty. She's fifty-one and looks it; I wouldn't have it any other way. What I meant by saying she was more or less naked was that spread across her nakedness were strands of cooked spaghetti, interspersed with bacon bits and lumps of yellow cheese. It was a dainty sight.

She smiled at me. "I don't have a knife or fork," she said.

"I guess I'll have to make do," I told her as I began to unbutton my shirt.

The Queen of Softness was offering me a home-cooked meal and I decided to partake.

7

On Tuesday morning I was groggy from lack of sleep. My midnight snack had continued for several hours and I felt bloated. Hadn't my mother always warned me not to chow down before bedtime? It was the morning of Bernard Logan's funeral, which was being held at ten o'clock. I put on my darkest gray suit and red silk tie. Charlie himself was spending the day at the courthouse with his Walkman and deck of cards. I had a poppy-seed bagel and coffee at Bruegger's Bagel Bakery, then walked down Broadway to the Bethesda Episcopal Church on Washington Street behind Charlie's mother's hotel. It was another sunny spring morning and several of the more upscale shops had window boxes full of tulips.

The church was packed. It was the first sense I really had of Logan's importance in horse circles, or maybe they were just a clubby bunch. Republicans love funerals; Democrats love births: accomplishment versus potential. Like the mayor was there and Harvey L. Peterson, Commissioner of Public Safety, who had been Charlie's boss in his old unredeemed days. I even saw two of Charlie's wealthy cousins. I guess funerals are important to Republicans because most of them believe that death can't happen to them and so they constantly need these grim reminders. I even saw tears in people's eyes,

but whether they were tears specifically for Bernard Logan
or for the more abstract idea that death was loose in the
world, I do not know.

An organist was dolefully cranking out Buxtehude and
people took their seats. Donald Croteau, Carl Logan and
Brenda Stanley all sat in front but they didn't sit together.
Croteau sat with Frankie Faber. He kept leaning over, whis-
pering to Faber, and then grinning. He looked chipper. The
guy he hated was at last in a box. Carl looked sad and Brenda
looked a thousand miles away. At least she wasn't sitting
with Randall Hanks who was seated back a few rows. I didn't
see McClintock but assumed I had missed him in the crowd.
Charlie's cousins looked at me, then wrinkled their noses and
looked away. Chief Peterson looked at me, then rolled his
eyes and looked away. Randall Hanks looked at me, then
appeared to grind his teeth. There is a real pleasure in knowing that wherever you go you will be unwelcome. I saw Arnette Stroud and he smiled. I had to remember to get the
newspaper.

The funeral gave me a context for Bernard Logan's life
that I hadn't had before: his place in society, his place in the
world of racing. Croteau had wanted to obliterate him, but
he might not have killed him. Brenda and Hanks had wanted
him gone, but they might not have killed him. Carl Logan
stood to inherit a lot of money from his father, but he might
not have killed them. Were there others? Frankie Faber was
possibly involved in a questionable deal that had cost Logan
three good horses in some claiming races. If Logan had been
suspicious, then maybe Faber had a motive. McClintock possibly wanted to help Carl, while also solidifying his own
position at the farm. After all, Hanks had accused him. Were
there more suspects?

Looking around the crowded church I saw a number of
the stable hands: Louie, who worried about the millennium,

Paul Something, whose broken arm was in a dark blue hospital sling, and there was even the kid who I had hired to catch the rats. Why wasn't he doing his job? It seemed that nobody was left at Battlefield Farms to hold down the fort. I decided to drive out and prowl around. Perhaps I would find another cattle prod. At least there would be no one to interfere with me.

Before retrieving the Mercedes, I grabbed a copy of the *Saratogian* and read Stroud's column as I stood next to the newspaper box, which I kept propped open with my foot. I could have kissed him. "Local Man Believes in Blood Sacrifice" read the headline.

"Last night, in one of Saratoga's most popular watering troughs, a fellow citizen who I will refer to only as Vic told me that he believed in sacrificing twelve-year-old virgins for purposes of witchcraft and devilry. With his tongue loosened from too much Guinness, and staggering at the bar, he described in gory detail how he has already sacrificed roosters and other small animals in order to cause injury to people he dislikes. Isn't there something to be done about this debasement of cultural values? Must our children always be in jeopardy?"

I was so pleased that I took five more copies of the paper out of the box before I let it slam shut. True, I didn't like that business about staggering at the bar and too much Guinness, but even such a false description would suit my purposes. Stroud described me as "a big overweight fellow in his mid-sixties with frizzy gray hair that stuck out in all directions and a nose turned vermillion from excessive drink." Never once did he call me handsome, but that too could be forgiven. The man had done me a favor the likes of which only a mother could have accomplished. I kept reading Stroud's column as I drove out to Battlefield Farms and the Mercedes zigzagged along the pavement. What a happy day!

Reaching the farm, I drove up the hill to the big ranch house, then drove around back to the parking lot, where there was only one other car. Horses were out in the fields and other horses were sticking their heads over the bottom doors of their stalls in the shed rows wondering where all the folks had gone. The two golden retrievers came bouncing around the corner of the greenhouse in order to get mud and dog spit on my clothes but I drove them away with shouts and curses. A small Latin-looking guy came strolling out of the greenhouse with a watering can to ask my business. I had seen him before but we'd never spoken. For these occasions I kept in my glove box an alligator-skin wallet with a brass shield that has the word "Detective" stamped across it. I had half a dozen of these babies made up a few years ago and they have always proved useful.

I showed him the shield. "I'm investigating," I said.

"Okay," he said, "you need any help, you let me know." He smiled, showing me a mouthful of white teeth. I smiled back, showing him my gold ones.

"How come you didn't go to the funeral?" I asked.

"Mr. Logan, he was most at peace when he worked with his orchids. I feel his spirit in the greenhouse, not in Saratoga."

"You liked the guy?"

The gardener gave me a big smile. "I liked how he liked his flowers."

We grinned at each other like the Cisco Kid and Pablo, then I gave him a wave and strolled off across the yard. I tried Randall Hanks's office first. The door was open and the room was empty. Although the belly drawer on his desk was locked, I jimmied it and proceeded to look through his papers. Most of the stuff was dull and business-related, but there were also a few short letters from Brenda Stanley—"Sweetheart, meet me at midnight near Duckfeather's stall. My body burns for you." There was a lot of stuff like that and I felt that Brenda could have easily benefited from a creative writing course on how to write love letters. Compared to my love letters, hers were very rudimentary. No references to specific body parts or what one planned to do with those body parts, no mention of peripheral apparatus—vibrators, ticklers, love-cuffs. The letters were altogether pedestrian.

The only bit of writing that stirred my blood was the following: "Soon we will be free of him and be together whenever we choose." I wondered if this was the letter that Logan had told me about. The freedom that she promised could suggest murder or simply departure; whatever the case, it was a clue. I pocketed the letter in order to show it to Charlie. At the back of the belly drawer was a loaded snub-nosed .38. It was dusty and, sniffing the barrel, I decided it had last been fired when Truman was president.

I tried Croteau's house next. I wanted to see if it was really the human wasteland that it had seemed the previous day. I looked through the window of the garage first. There was the Porsche covered with a white drop cloth to keep the ants from tramping all over its pristine surface. Under the cloth it had the shape of an anal suppository. I went around to the front of the house. The door was unlocked and I pushed it open. I was touched by the level of trust at Battlefield Farms. Considering how everybody wanted to murder everybody else, no one seemed to have the least concern for thievery. Charlie hated it when I went on these searches. He called them illegal. But for me they were a stimulating part of the job. I loved looking in people's sock drawers and medicine cabinets. I would love to be invisible and peek into their lives: see their nocturnal habits and how they eat their food when they are alone.

Croteau was pathologically neat. If you could only see how carefully he folded his pristine white jockey shorts in the top drawer of his bureau, then you would be forced to had tried to cheer him up with a string of cop jokes. For the most part state cops are pretty good guys, although they exercise too much and they lack a sense of humor. Like they spend all their free time on cross-country ski machines and it sweats the jokes right out of them. Also you sometimes feel that in their heart of hearts, they would prefer a military government. Who can blame them, right? I wouldn't mind a military government myself as long as I could be boss general with a junta of my choosing.

A uniformed state cop had joined me at the door and then Stachek came loping across the yard. He was in his forties and has muscles instead of heart. There was nothing soft about him and I wondered how his wife hung on during their nights of connubial bliss. It must have been like sleeping with the bronze statue of Rodin's *Thinker*. All these state investigators have been touchy of late because of a state guy in Ithaca who was sent up for faking evidence. Like he knew the crooks were guilty so why waste time looking for real evidence when he could doctor a few fingerprints? It has made the rest of the state cops even fussier and nit-pickier than usual. They've even been putting extra starch in their neckties. Stachek wore a brown suit. He had that singed and sooty look that you find on some Eastern Europeans: thick black eyebrows, a perpetual five-o'clock shadow and little smudges under his cheekbones. He had short black hair that came to a point in the middle of his forehead. That point seemed to function like a cowcatcher on a steam locomotive: it was what Stachek used to push himself into the world.

"Did you go inside?" he asked me. Maybe you notice that he didn't say Hello or How have you been?

"Yup."

"Did you touch anything?"

"Just the phone."

"How d'you know he's dead?"

agree that what we had before us was a sick man. The bathroom was immaculate and he kept his toothbrush in a little glass box with brass hinges. Although there was a TV in the bedroom, it was small and stoical. There were lots of vitamins in the medicine cabinet, plus stuff like garlic pills. No books or magazines, not even any condoms. It occurred to me that he might be deep into Transcendental Meditation and spend all his free time trying to levitate. The furniture in the living room was covered with plastic. It appeared virginal and unsat-on. Rummaging through the kitchen, I discovered that his cooking consisted of frozen dinners and a microwave oven. The refrigerator was full of bottles of Poland Spring Water. No ice cream, no cookies or cake, nothing nice. Like when he wanted to punish himself, he had dinner.

On the other side of the living room was a small office with a desk and two file cabinets. I spent about half an hour going through his papers. There were no letters or anything personal. In the L section was a file marked "Laurel Hill Farms." It attracted my attention because I had never heard of the place. The papers in the file contained mostly boring numbers, but there were also inventories, the names of horses, monies paid out, monies received. It looked like some kind of investment property. I mention the file only because it became important later on.

It was past eleven-thirty by the time I got out of Croteau's house. I figured I only had a short time before people started coming back from the funeral and I wanted to check out Frankie Faber's office in the horse barn. I hoped to learn more about those horses that had been recently claimed. As I hurried to the barn, the golden retrievers saw me and decided I wanted to frolic and romp, so I had shout at them some more. They weren't bad dogs as far as dogs go, but for me dogs don't go very far.

Faber's office was around the side of the barn. Since he

was boss of the horses, it was a substantial room and meant to impress visitors. Like it had a leather couch. Pictures of winning horses covered the walls. Their display so completely took my attention that it was a few seconds before I realized that someone was seated at Faber's desk. Then I realized he was not sitting but lying and maybe sleeping. It was Neil McClintock. Then I realized he wasn't sleeping, he was dead.

McClintock was in the desk chair and his head and torso were lying forward over the blotter. He wore a red shirt and there was so much blood that at first it seemed to have come from the shirt itself. In his left hand was a pistol. I didn't bother to sniff it. On the wall behind him was a round splotch of blood and brain bits, hair and bone. There was a yellow pencil by his right hand and at the edge of the blotter, nearly encircled by a pool of blood, was scrawled the word "Sorry." McClintock's head lay in the blood and his salt-and-pepper beard and mustache were full of it. I could only see his right eye. It was open and very blue. It seemed thoughtful but empty of ideas. I had liked McClintock, moderately. I remembered being concerned about his blood pressure and feeling that he was destined for an early stroke. It looked like I had been mistaken about his possible upcoming health problems.

The telephone on the corner of the desk was free of blood. I used it to call the state cops. Just as I hung up, I heard the first cars coming back from the funeral. I guessed there would be another funeral very shortly, although perhaps not so well attended as Bernard Logan's, but I bet McClintock had more friends. My stomach told me that it wanted me to take it someplace so it could throw up. I told my stomach to shut up.

• • •

Within half an hour the state cops were swarming all over the place and more were arriving every minute. Every one of them was in a hurry. At the same time, cars of stable hands were returning from the funeral. These guys were a trifle poky. Right away a major law of physics was being violated: the one that says two objects cannot occupy the same place at the same time. It was so bad they had to get a cop out there to direct traffic. None of the people from the farm had any idea what had happened and they all wore what-what? expressions.

I stood by the door of Faber's office and wouldn't let anybody in. Carl Logan stood with me in his dark suit. He was weeping, a loud choking noise that almost had me weeping as well, and I could feel a lump in my throat. I hate to weep. I find it an insult to my positive attitude toward life. It seems like a surrender to the general sadness that is always lurking in the corners of the world. Someday, when I have a free moment, I will have my tear ducts surgically removed.

Carl had been one of the first people back from the funeral. He said he had been worried about McClintock because he hadn't been at the church.

"Had he been depressed," I had asked, "or had he seemed anxious?"

"No, none of that. He was going to meet me and we were going to have lunch in town." Logan had that slapped look that people get when someone near to them dies unexpectedly. Like death is the constant player, the guy who invents the games and makes the rules, yet we treat it as an interloper, as if it were the stranger and not the guy who owns the house.

"Why didn't he ride in with you?"

"He said he had some last-minute business to take care of and he didn't want to make me late."

The state cop in charge was a lieutenant named Stachek. I didn't remember his first name, maybe he didn't have one. I had met him before with Charlie on an arson case and he was not a member of the Vic Plotz Fan Club, even though

"Half his brains are competing with the art work on the wall."

"Don't go away," said Stachek.

He entered the office and some other state cops followed him. I had started to mosey off when the uniformed cop at the door said, "You heard what he told you."

"I'll be on the grounds," I said.

"He wants you here."

"I gotta take a leak."

This embarrassed the copper. He was a young guy with eyebrows that went up and down every few seconds. "Be sure you come right back," he said.

"I promise, officer."

I had seen Frankie Faber over near the oak tree by the shed row and I wanted to talk to him. His coiffed rock-and-roll haircut made him stand out like a dandelion in a cereal bowl. He was with a couple of stable hands, one of them being the kid who was catching me the rats. They were all wearing coats and ties from the funeral and had solemn expressions. I spoke to the kid first. "You had any luck for me?"

"I got ten so far. I used a butterfly net like you said."

"Hot damn. Try and get some more, will you?"

"Just let me change my clothes." The kid happily trotted away. Catching rats made far more sense to him than death and taxes. It was a project with a clear goal and sensible purpose. The rest of life was just a mystery.

Frankie Faber took my arm, but lightly, not meaning offense. "He's dead on my desk?" He was sipping on a Budweiser and looked like he needed it.

"Right across the blotter."

"Shot himself?"

"Looks that way."

"Jeez, I never would have thought it." Faber stood there

rubbing his cheek as if wondering whether he needed a shave. He must have had a hard time as a jock. At five-seven or so he was almost too tall and had probably spent his days starving and puking. "You think he was the one who made Triclops go crazy?" he asked. His tone of voice was almost hopeful.

"I don't know," I said. "I guess he could have done it."

But stated like that I realized I didn't believe for one moment that McClintock had tortured the horse with a cattle prod and a bag full of rats. McClintock's operating emotion had been indignation, which implied, in the shady background, a sense of justice, which might be distorted but which wouldn't include tormenting a horse. Or at least that was how it seemed to me.

I was also impressed that Faber seemed to know everything about how Triclops had been driven crazy with the rats and how Logan's death hadn't been an accident. But I supposed everybody knew it. People talked and it was all over the farm.

The other stable hands had wandered off and Faber and I were by ourselves. "I wanted to ask you," I said, "about those horses that got claimed this past month or so down at Belmont."

Faber took a step back and squinched his eyes at me. If I'd said I wanted to give him an enema, he couldn't have looked any more distressed. "I don't know what you're talking about."

"Sure you do. Three of Logan's best horses were put in races way below their class and someone snapped them up. Why'd you put them in those races?"

"They weren't his best horses," said Faber, trying to crank up his indignation. "It was a mistake, that's all. They'd all been running badly. That kind of thing happens all the time."

"Who claimed them?"

"I have no idea." He squinched his eyes some more and his rock-and-roll hairdo bobbed up and down.

Although he had suddenly remembered the horses in question, Frankie still struck me as a guy for whom truth was only an option, like he had a bag of answers and he just had to reach in and grab a pretty one.

"Then why did old man Logan feel you were ripping him off?"

"He never did! He never said anything to me!"

It wasn't that Frankie was physically frightened, but he clearly felt I could hurt him. Maybe I could fix it so he lost his license; maybe I could put him in jail. I figured I had him on the run but right then I was rudely interrupted by one of the state cops.

"Lieutenant Stachek wants you, sir."

I get called "sir" so rarely that I hardly knew who he was talking to, but after a second I caught on.

"Tell him I'm busy."

"He said no excuses, sir."

The cop stood waiting with his hard cop face so I gave it up and followed him back toward the horse barn. Frankie Faber had been relieved by the interruption and I knew when I spoke to him again he would have a tidy little story. I glanced back and saw him happily sucking on his Budweiser.

Stachek met me at the door of the office. In his right hand he held a folded aluminum armchair with green webbing. He gave his wrist a flick and the chair snapped open. He set it against the wall. "I don't want you muddying the water," he told me. "Stay here or I'll have you cuffed."

"It might rain," I said.

We both looked at the sky. There were no clouds.

"What about lunch?" I asked.

Stachek ignored me and went back into the office.

The young state cop with the eyebrows looked at me reproachfully. "You never had to pee," he said.

"I internalized it," I said.

• • •

I spent a couple of hours in that chair working on my tan. It was peaceful. Until late in the afternoon cops ran back and forth doing the kind of stuff cops do when they have a dead body. They have so much fun with it that I'm surprised they don't scrag a few extra people themselves just so they can indulge in these pleasures more often. Guys came with big lights, guys came with cameras and fingerprint equipment and mysterious boxes. Guys ran around with measuring tapes and clipboards. Around two o'clock McClintock's body was taken away in an ambulance. A bunch of stable hands came out of the shed rows to watch. They were a depressed lot and I had the sense that McClintock had been a popular guy, despite his temper.

Right after that a sergeant named Culver took me over to Hanks's office to get my statement. Hanks himself was nowhere in sight. Sergeant Culver was a solid block of hardwood dressed in a tan polyester suit. Maybe he was forty. He asked what I was doing at the farm and how I had happened to find the body and what my relationship had been to the deceased. He seemed to have trouble understanding my role in the general proceedings.

"You know how a cook cooks?" I asked. "And how a runner runs and a judge judges? Well, an investigator investigates. I've been investigating."

"Investigating what?"

"Logan's murder."

"But he was killed by a horse."

"Ah," I said, "but who activated the horse? That's what I've been investigating. Who held the horse over his head and beat Logan to death with it?"

Sergeant Culver didn't understand my entertaining remarks but he wrote them all down. He wrote a lot, like he was one of those guys who feels the world doesn't exist until he puts it into language. I figured if he kept writing like this, then by the time he was my age he'd have a barn full of notes. I gave him a brief and sanitized version of events as I knew them, but it was a mystery, right? I mean, who knew why Logan got scragged?

After McClintock's body was removed, Stachek began talking to the principals. He took them into Faber's office so they could see the blood and brain bits and ideally suffer a crisis of conscience and confess to the shooting of President Kennedy and the sinking of the *Titanic*. When they came out, they looked a little pale. First he talked to Carl Logan, then to Brenda Stanley, then Hanks, then Croteau, then Frankie Faber. But none of them suffered so much as to spill the beans, whatever beans were around to spill. A couple of sergeants, including the one who had taken my statement, were talking to the stable hands. What started getting me angry was that Stachek still hadn't talked to me, hadn't put my words before all the others, because even if I didn't know who had done what, I knew what was going on better than anyone else. I was also angry because I was hungry. It was nearly four o'clock and I hadn't had lunch. I asked the uniformed cop if I couldn't get a Coke and a bag of chips, maybe a candy bar, from the machines in the room where the stable hands hung out.

"You abused your privileges earlier," he told me. "You should have thought of that before."

"Do you ever masturbate?" I asked him. "I mean, really jack off?"

The copper refused to answer but a pretty blush suffused his cheeks.

"Do you have warts on your palms? Come on, let me see. I bet they're all hairy."

"You're disgusting," said the trooper.

So I sat. Now and then I saw the young stable hand with the butterfly net prowling around the shed rows and the barns. Once he waved to me. "Two more!" he called.

"Great work!" I answered.

Without my cellular phone, I couldn't even find out how the stock market was doing. I couldn't even call the Queen of Softness! As the day advanced, I found myself coming to an end of my inner resources. By the time Stachek decided to see me around five o'clock, I was as hot under the collar as Mount St. Helens dressed in a tuxedo.

Stachek invited me into Faber's office. The bloodstains on the walls were dry by now and had turned brown.

"What the fuck you been keeping me out there for?" I said. "I could have split this case wide open hours ago. Your professional jealousy makes me sick."

"You know I could have you booked as an accessory after the fact?" Stachek stood by the desk with his legs apart and his hands joined behind his back, like he had seen cops pose on TV cop shows. The smudges under his cheekbones made him look as if someone had been flicking soot balls at him.

"Up your snout," I said.

"Neither you nor Bradshaw reported that rat cage above the horse's stall. Failure to disclose important evidence could get you in a lot of trouble."

"Go piss up a rope." I sat down on the leather couch. There was no way that I was going to let Stachek intimidate me. "Both Charlie and me told the investigator Saturday morning that Logan had come to the office worried that someone wanted to scrag him. Do you think that meant anything to the guy? Oh no, he figured he'd caught the horse red-handed, or maybe red-hoofed, and he wasn't going to cut into his lunch hour by widening the investigation. You book me for anything and I'll tell such a story of state cop incompetence that you'll have trouble getting a job as a crossing guard at a ghetto grade school. You don't like the fact we've been here? Tough knee socks! You weren't about to do it and we were getting paid. Now what about McClintock, did he shoot himself or not?"

Stachek dangled unhappily from the horns of a moral dilemma. He wanted to hit me but he knew he wasn't supposed to. One, I was old. Two, I was a law-abiding taxpayer. Three, I'm the kind of guy who calls his lawyer fast. He stood facing me and I listened to his heart beat. If he wanted to hear any more nasty cracks I had trunks and trunks full of them. Like I wrote the textbook on nasty cracks. At last he took a deep breath, pursed his lips and exhaled with a windy sighing sound.

"The muzzle of the gun wasn't pressed against his head," said Stachek, "and the fingerprints are smudgy. He could have shot himself, but maybe not."

"What about the handwriting on the 'Sorry'?"

"It's just a scrawl. Again, maybe he did it and maybe he didn't."

"Did anybody see him come in here?"

"Everybody says no. They were at the funeral."

"Do you know who left last or anything like that?"

"No. They left at different times and took different roads. Nine cars left from here. Now it's my turn to ask questions."

"Shoot."

"Why'd you come back here early?"

"I wanted to poke around without being interrupted."

"Did anybody see you?"

"Only that guy working in the greenhouse and the two golden retrievers. I signed their autograph book."

"Weren't you worried about trespassing?" Stachek lowered his head slightly so that the sharp point of black hair bisecting his forehead gestured threateningly in my direction.

"Not so I'd lose any sleep over it." I couldn't believe he was serious, but some of these state guys drive the speed limit, don't fudge on their taxes and remember their wives' birthdays: all sorts of amazing stuff.

"The lab took away the cage that Bradshaw found. They'll check it for rat hairs."

"That'll be fun for them. You plan to make an arrest anytime soon?"

"At the moment it looks as if McClintock murdered his employer and then took his own life."

"You don't believe that," I said. "Only an idiot would believe it."

"Perhaps. But that's what somebody wants us to believe."

"Who?" I asked.

So for the next half hour Stachek and I went around and around. Who had motive, who had opportunity. Some stuff I kept back, like why did Stachek need to know about those claiming races? Still, we talked about everybody and by the end I was almost willing to accept that McClintock had killed his boss and then scragged himself. It was easier that way and I still hadn't had lunch. But I had liked McClintock and that was the only thing which kept me honest.

"Go get Bradshaw," said Stachek at last. "Get him or I'll pull him in."

"Falling back on the old tough-guy role, are you?" I said. "Every cop's got to show his true colors."

"Just get him." There was a weary note in Stachek's voice that almost touched my heart.

As I walked back to my car, I saw Randall Hanks coming out of Logan's house. I called to him, "Hey, Hanks!" I wanted to ask him about that love letter I still had in my pocket.

When he saw me, Hanks spun on his heel and went back inside. So much for being Mr. Popularity. I considered following him but I didn't want to keep Stachek waiting. Who am I kidding? It was past five-thirty and I was ready to eat my shoe soles. Charlie's house on the lake was the nearest place where I could find food. Even if Charlie wasn't home, I planned to break in.

Just as I was getting into my car, Eddie Gillespie tooled into the parking lot in his fancy red Ford pickup with double chrome pipes. He skidded to a stop and hopped out of the cab. Then he put his fingers to his nose and pinched his nostrils.

"Smells," he said.

"Horse poop," I said.

"I don't like it," he said.

"You're too refined, Eddie. You should get a job with the ballet."

He considered that. It seemed to appeal to him. He wore black pants, a white shirt and a black leather jacket. He has long curly black locks which are artificially tousled. It's amazing. He can toss his head and send his hair into any one of a dozen prearranged styles or patterns. It's like the signals birds send to each other. He can do this in a bar and the women flock to him and make pigeon noises.

"What're you doing here, Eddie?"

"Charlie gave me a little job."

"What kind of job?"

Eddie put his finger to his lips. "I can't tell. It's Charlie's secret."

I considered tossing a big rock at his truck. "How's the wife, Eddie? Still beating you up?"

She had kicked him once and I didn't let him forget it.

"You're mean," he said.

• • •

I got to say that I hit Charlie's refrigerator like the plague of locusts hit Egypt. Charlie was there but I pushed him aside. I dug, I burrowed, I ate. One of the nice things about Charlie is that he likes snacks: Cheez Doodles and chocolate-chip ice cream. I made a sandwich with peanut butter, salami and Swiss cheese and I thought I'd have to make another. I didn't chew, I just inhaled deeply.

"Feeling a little hungry?" asked Charlie, standing in the doorway of the kitchen. He had changed out of his suit and wore khakis with paint stains and a blue Red Sox sweatshirt. His porkpie hat was set at a jaunty angle on his scalp.

"Damn coppers have been starving me out of envy for my fine figure," I said.

"What coppers?"

"The coppers who showed up because of McClintock's murder or suicide, they can't decide which."

"McClintock?"

"Oh, you didn't hear, did you?" Through all this I spoke with my mouth stuffed with food. With each word I sprayed food particles around the kitchen: little digestible mortar shells for the ants.

"Dammit, Victor, you know I don't know anything about it. Tell me what happened."

"How was jury duty?"

"I got disqualified for the Sunoco break-in case because it turns out that my cousin James owns the property. Tomorrow they got a case about a dog bite and the lawyers will decide if they want me or not. I can promise they won't."

"Tut-tut, Charlie, where's your civic duty?"

"Tell about McClintock or you won't get any chocolate fudge ripple ice cream."

So I told him what I knew.

8

So around six-thirty Charlie and I drove back to Battlefield Farms. By now I knew the road so well I could have done it blindfolded. People were home from work and puttering in their yards: mowing them, raking them, seeding them. Kids were playing catch; moms were on their knees in the flower beds; dads were tooling around on tractor mowers. There is something about a warm evening in May with birds flapping overhead holding bits of string in their beaks that makes me consider having a family again. Of course, it takes half a nanosecond for me to realize it is too late and then the regrets set in. They aren't big regrets and no tears get shed, but I think how I'd like to be roaring up and down on a power mower as my wife pruned the tulips and my kids threw a ball around. I even think about what kind of dog I'd get, even though I hate dogs. This kind of sentimental thinking lasts only until I slap myself across the chops and tell myself to shape up: maybe about a minute. I don't tell Charlie what's been on my mind. Better to have him think I'm tough.

"By the way, Victor," said Charlie after a minute, "I saw a terrible article about you today in the *Saratogian*."

"Oh yeah. Stroud. Ha, ha." I didn't make a real laugh, just a pretend laugh.

"Did you really tell him that stuff?" Charlie's tone of voice was the same he might have used for: Did you really run down a nun with a motorcycle?

"Sure. I mean, he cranked it up a little, but I gave him the basics." The smell of cut grass drifted through the open windows. I could have breathed it all day and night.

"But why?" persisted Charlie. "Are you really involved with blood sacrifice?"

"Never touch the stuff. It gives me pimples."

"Then why'd you tell him all that garbage? You know what people are going to think about you?"

"Hey, Charlie, as far as I'm concerned that is one useful article. I worked for it and my labors were handsomely rewarded. I mean, it might be a problem if I had a reputation to lose, but I don't. Consequently, since nothing more can be taken away from me, then I can only be added to, which means I hope that article will wind up doing me a world of good."

"Sometimes I just don't understand you," said Charlie. He said this like he might say that he didn't understand Jean-Paul Sartre, meaning that it wasn't meant to be insulting.

"Don't worry, pal. I understand me well enough for both of us. All this will become clear at the proper time."

Charlie was still scratching his head so I changed the subject. "Have you ever heard of Laurel Hill Farms?" I asked.

"No, should I have?"

"Donald Croteau had a file labeled with that name. It had lots of numbers, buyings and sellings, accounts received and payable. I wondered if you knew anything about it."

"Nothing. Were you poking around in his house?" The shadow in his voice was like a dark cloud lurking in the distance.

"Just a tad," I said.

"You wouldn't like jail, Victor, the food's no good."

"Life on the edge, Charlie, it makes the heart beat fast."

"I thought you kept the Queen of Softness for that."

"She's only for romance and fast-food excursions," I said. "But speaking of romance, I got a letter for you. Brenda wrote it to Randall Hanks." I fished the letter out of the inside pocket of my suitcoat.

Charlie took it from my hand. "Did you steal this too?"

"Let's say I liberated it. Come on, Charlie, don't be such a Boy Scout. We're detectives."

"That doesn't mean we're above the law," he said in a choirboy sort of voice. Then he began reading the letter. I waited for him to get to the important sentence: "Soon we will be free of him and be together whenever we choose."

"Not bad," said Charlie, after a minute. "Have you talked to either of them about this?"

We were getting close to the farm. I could see the big white ranch house just at the top of the next hill. Cows in the fields were ambling toward their barns.

"I wanted to try Hanks first, but he's been avoiding me."

"Try and find him while I talk to Lieutenant Stachek." Charlie gave me back the letter.

"By the way," I asked, "what do you have Goofy Gillespie doing? He was acting like he was carrying atomic secrets."

Charlie grinned. "I wanted him to talk to all the stable hands about who might have put the rattrap above Triclops's stall," said Charlie. "But mostly I wanted him to call attention to himself and make people nervous."

"He'll do that well enough," I said. "Did he get a line on where all those rats came from?"

"Not really. The places that sell rats don't sell them to

individuals, only to labs and actual scientists. So Eddie will start checking nearby colleges and universities tomorrow."

•   ●   •

By the time we got to Battlefield Farms, a lot of the state cops had packed up and left. Stachek stood cooling his heels in the parking lot, talking to Carl Logan, who still looked sad. It gave him a little crease on his handsome forehead between his eyebrows. When Stachek saw my Mercedes he glared at me in order to suggest that I had been dawdling and might be in need of official chastisement. I gave him a big smile to show him how much I admired his professional copper ways. He ignored the smile and shook hands with Charlie. He obviously liked Charlie and was pleased to see him.

"So you been on jury duty?" said Stachek as if this were a big joke.

"Didn't Victor tell you?" said Charlie. "I'm on the panel. I hang around just waiting to be disqualified."

We stood in the parking lot. Carl remained off to the side watching us, but he seemed friendly, like we were all chums.

"Your friend Plotz has told me all sorts of stuff," said Stachek, "but I don't know what's true and what's false."

"You just don't know how to read him," said Charlie, giving me a wink.

"I was about to try Braille," said Stachek.

I can't tell you how much I dislike the type of conversation that might be called Let's Rag on Vic Plotz. But instead of pinning both of these bozos to the mat with a few choice remarks, I joined Carl instead. He had changed out of his funeral duds into jeans and a blue denim shirt.

"Anything new?" I asked him, leading him away.

"The cops haven't discovered anything, if that's what you mean. Who's that guy with the fancy hair who says he is working for Bradshaw? Says his name's Gillespie. He's getting some of the stable hands pretty irritated with his questions."

"He's what they call a catalyst," I said. "Charlie will sometimes toss him into a situation in order to cause a chemical reaction." We were now over on the grass, about twenty feet from Charlie and Stachek. I saw several men over by the shed rows fussing with some horses but they were no one I recognized. The two golden retrievers were racing around trying to gnaw each other's ears. They were an irresponsible lot.

"Randall Hanks was talking to some of the guys," said Logan, "and this Gillespie came hurrying up and asked which one was responsible for McClintock's murder. I thought Hanks was going to hit him."

"Yup, that's how Eddie operates. It's the opposite of finesse and subtlety: the baseball-bat-instead-of-a-toothpick approach. It's meant to drive the criminal out of hiding."

"Does it work?" asked Logan.

"Not unless you have a terrifically stupid criminal," I said. "Where's Hanks now?"

"I haven't seen him."

"By the way, have you ever heard of someplace called Laurel Hill Farms?"

"No, why?"

"Just a name I had on my mind. You think Hanks could be in the big house?"

"I have no idea." He was a nice kid but he was getting sick of my questions.

"I think I'll go check," I said.

I walked up the front steps of the house and leaned on the doorbell. It was one of those trick doorbells and it played "The Yellow Rose of Texas." I figured I would only need to hear it about twice before I'd want to rip the whole thing out of the wall. Even "Havah Nagela" would become tedious.

After a few minutes Brenda Stanley opened up. She was wearing a Hard Rock Café T-shirt that fit her like the apple peel fits the apple. I decided I needed to be kindly and solicitous.

"I just wanted to know how you were," I said.

She looked up at me from under her blond eyelashes as if she wanted to believe me but found it difficult. Then she stood aside to let me in.

"Do the police think Neil shot himself?" she asked, hoping it was true.

"No, they don't."

She turned away and her pretty face became hard. "When will it stop?" she said.

"When will what stop?"

She smiled and shook her head. "I'm just terribly frightened."

For a moment I considered putting my arm around her but I didn't want to push my luck. We were standing in the hall. On the walls were eighteenth-century English prints of racing horses: elongated bodies and red-coated jockeys. "If it turns out that somebody murdered McClintock," I asked, "do you have any ideas about who it might be?"

She opened her eyes very wide in a way that was meant to indicate that she was telling the truth. "Absolutely none."

"Did you ever hear of a place called Laurel Hill Farms?"

"No, is it important I have?"

"I don't know. It's just my trick question for the day."

"I don't think I've ever heard of it." The line of her short blond hair so precisely matched the line of her jaw that I wished I had a ruler in order to make exact calculations.

"By the way," I asked, making my voice a little gruffer, "is Randall here? I need to talk to him."

A trace of anxiety peeked out of her eyes. "I haven't seen him for a while. Is it something I can help you with?"

I considered showing her the love letter, but then changed my mind. She was too clever and could cover up too easily. With Hanks I stood a better chance. It was the difference between a good liar and a bad liar.

"Nah," I said, "it's boys' business."

She smiled as if she knew all about boys' business. As I opened the door to leave, she said, "I appreciate your concern, Victor. You're one of the few good things that has happened recently."

She wasn't really flirting, but she understood that I was predisposed to the charms of the shorter sex. I gave her a Jolly Roger smile, but actually I felt regretful. I have never liked people who think they can wind me around their fingers with a few sweet words. Even if Brenda had invited me to join her atop a hay bale, I would be forced to turn her down. Like it wouldn't be the purity of my soul, nor the beef torpedo of my body that would be tweaking her interest, but the fact that I might do her a favor in return.

I left Brenda, meaning to look for her paramour, the rugged Randall Hanks. I had the sense that I would only have to show him the letter and he would crumple and confess. Of course, events don't happen like that, but it is the hyperbole of the imaginative life that helps us accept the lackluster of the real. It was just sunset and I noticed a light in the greenhouse so I wandered over. The greenhouse was connected to the big house by a covered walkway, maybe about eight feet long, which led to a rear door. When I entered the greenhouse, the temperature rose about twenty degrees and the humidity increased thirty percent. The air felt like a warm wet washcloth which someone has sprayed with expensive perfume. The Latin-looking guy who I had seen earlier was bent over a lavender-colored orchid. I don't know what he was doing, maybe checking it for ear mites.

He glanced up and gave me a third-world grin: no sub-terfuge but no deep feeling. "You like orchids?" he asked me.

"Not particularly," I said, "but I like proms."

He watched that one go by and blinked. He had long thick eyelashes and when he blinked I felt I should hear a click. "Mr. Logan, he loved orchids. I think he loved them more than horses."

"They're easier to pin to a girl's dress," I said.

To tell you the truth, I wasn't much interested in the orchids. I was looking for Hanks and was just glancing around, but the gardener was a pleasant bundle of goods and there was something about the smell and high humidity of the greenhouse that made it seem like another world so I found myself dawdling.

"Logan spent a lot of time here, did he?" I asked. The greenhouse was about thirty feet by twenty feet with an aisle on either side. Along the outside walls were long tables with plants and another wider table was in the center. Some of the plants were climbers and went right up to the glass roof.

"In the past year, Mr. Logan spent lots of time here. Maybe twenty hours a week, maybe more. It took his mind off his troubles." The gardener wore green pants and a green workshirt. It made him look something like a plant himself. He was about forty-five and had the body of a steeplechase jockey.

"And what do you know about his troubles?"

"I know that outside that door his life grew much harder."

"That would also be true of a cockroach," I said. "Give me details."

"Outside that door he fought with everybody. In here, he didn't."

"Did he fight with his son, Carl?" I asked.

"No, he loved his son, but he and Carl disagreed."

"What'd they disagree about?"

"Carl wanted to go away and his father wanted him to stay here. Carl wanted to sell his part of the farm."

"Not to Croteau?" I asked. That would have given Donald Croteau half ownership.

"Carl wanted to leave and his father wouldn't buy his ten percent. Yes, he was thinking of selling it to Croteau." The gardener was holding a small trowel and when he spoke, he gestured with it as if sculpting the air.

"That must have upset the old guy," I said.

"When Mr. Logan came in here, he put those troubles away. He has flowers from all over the world: the Caribbean, Sri Lanka, Madagascar, Tahiti, Africa."

"Are they all orchids?"

"Mostly, but he has other tropicals as well. He had many books and read all the time."

"I wonder what will happen to the greenhouse now?"

The gardener touched his fingers to his lips and made a blowing noise. "It will go as the wind goes," he said. "Like all of us."

· ● ·

Outside, Stachek had left and Charlie was talking to some stable hands over by the shed rows. It was twilight and half a dozen bats were snarfing up the random bugs who had been on a variety of important errands until rudely interrupted by death.

I headed over toward the other shed row, which contained Hanks's office. Lights were on in Donald Croteau's small ranch house and I imagined him putting a little box of Slimfast food into the microwave. Later he might give his red Porsche a full body rub.

Hanks wasn't in his office, but Carl was nearby talking to Paul with the broken arm. Paul seemed unhappy and it looked like more was the matter than being temporarily crippled. When he saw me, Carl said good night to Paul and strolled over in my direction. He too had a seriousness that seemed on the edge of despair. For me the incidents at Battlefield Farms were a diversion from my normal life, but for Carl and the others, their world was being violently ripped to pieces. I let that thought sober me for a moment before my natural ebullience reasserted itself.

"What's wrong with Paul?" I asked. "Can't he pick his nose anymore?"

"A number of the guys are worried about the farm," said Logan. He pushed a hand through his black hair. "I mean, what's going to happen to it."

"The big future," I said.

Logan didn't answer. We walked along the shed row and he looked down at his feet. A quarter moon was dangling over the river to the east. One thinks of bad things happening in bad places, not in beautiful places like this one.

"By the way," I said, "you didn't tell me you were thinking of selling your part of the farm."

"My father's death has changed that. I'm not sure what I'm going to do now."

"Would you really have sold your ten percent of the farm to Croteau?"

"I wanted out. I mean, everybody here was quarreling and my father spent all his time in that damn greenhouse. I just didn't want to be here anymore."

"And what did your father want?"

"He wanted me to take over the farm, but there was no way that could happen unless Croteau sold me his forty percent and he refused to sell. My father would ask him and Donald would just smile and shake his head. My father only had to express a wish for anything and Donald would try to thwart it."

A horse stuck its head over the bottom half of a stall door and I scratched its nose. Its fur had a greasy feel. "What about Brenda's part of the farm?"

"She wanted a huge amount of money for it, over a quarter of a million, and she wanted a divorce. She felt pretty sure that my father would give it to her eventually, just to get rid of her. She and Hanks were increasingly blatant about their relationship. I felt she was doing that just to increase the pressure on my father to buy her out."

"Could Croteau have bought her out?"

"No. Although their nuptial agreement gave her twenty-five percent, she couldn't sell. Or rather, she couldn't sell it to anybody but my father during his lifetime."

"She said she'd been thinking of selling her portion to Croteau, which he could claim after your father's death."

"Yeah, I guess she could have done that."

We started walking again. The security light above the shed row blinked on and made Carl Logan's face look yellow. "So you were going to change your life by selling out to Croteau and leaving."

"It would have solved my problem, no one else's. But my father didn't like the farm anymore. If he could have gotten rid of the whole thing and moved to California, it wouldn't have mattered. But he didn't want to be beaten by Croteau and he didn't want to be beaten by Brenda Stanley. It wasn't love of Battlefield Farms that kept him here, it was pride."

"Could he have sold his own portion to Croteau or Brenda?"

"Perhaps legally, but Croteau wouldn't have bought it if he felt it was something my father wanted. And Brenda didn't have the money."

"What a happy family," I said. "Do you think Mc-Clintock could have killed your father just to break the stalemate?"

"I don't know," said Carl. "I can't believe it. Neil was angry at my father and felt he was wrecking the farm by doing nothing. But I can't believe he would have killed him."

We had paused by the corner of the shed row and I had started thinking about happiness and how it is mostly something that other folks seem to have when I saw the kid who was supposed to be catching me the rats come racing across the yard in our direction from the hay barn.

When he saw us, he veered toward us. "Mr. Hanks," he shouted, "Mr. Hanks is dead!"

The kid slid to a stop. He seemed all set to fly into a hundred pieces.

"What happened?" asked Logan.

"It was Triclops again. Triclops kicked him to death. He's in Triclops's stall."

Logan was already running in the direction of the hay barn. "Go tell the others," I told the kid. "And make sure you tell Mr. Bradshaw. In fact, tell him first."

I took off after Logan. If truth be told, I am not much of a runner. At most I could be called a hurrier. A rapid trot is about the best I can manage. Consequently, by the time I got to the middle of the yard, Logan had already entered the barn. By now all the security lights were lit and the buildings and trees and grass were bathed in yellow light. When I run, I can feel my belly bounce against my ribs and my leg bones rattle in their sockets. In fact, the whole corpus finds it a rude and humiliating experience.

When I entered the barn, Logan was already inside the box stall. Considering how hysterical Triclops had been after his previous episodes with rats, I was afraid that Carl might get himself stomped, which led me to trot faster than my body otherwise liked. Reaching the entrance to the stall, I found Logan holding Triclops by the halter. Randall Hanks lay on the straw on his stomach. His head was mushed to a red pulp and the straw around him was bloody. Triclops was certainly upset—his ears kept going back and forward and his eyes rolled around in his head—but he wasn't hysterical. When he tried to rear up, Logan pulled him down again.

"Can you tie him up outside the stall?" I asked. "The cops are going to want to come in here."

Logan led the horse into the feed passage just as a bunch of people ran into the barn, which caused a certain commotion, not to say shouting. Triclops was getting a reputation as bad as Bonnie and Clyde's. Hanks was sprawled in the center of the stall. He wore a dark blue blazer and blood-smeared tan pants. I knelt down by his body. Cut into his scalp and forehead was the impression of a horse's hoof with blood oozing and clotting around it. An eye was open but it wasn't registering anything, not even question marks. The body was warm but not very. All I knew for certain was that Randall Hanks was dead.

Charlie came running into the stall. He was puffing and out of breath. When he saw Hanks, his face got all wrinkled. "What a shame," he said. "Why'd he come in here in the first place?"

"He didn't confide in me," I said.

"The police should be on their way." Charlie knelt down by the body and looked at the wounds on Hanks's head. Charlie's porkpie hat rolled into the straw and I picked it up for him.

Half a dozen people were crowded at the entrance of the stall. I could hear Triclops whinnying and nervously stamping his feet. I wondered if there was blood on his hooves or white stockings. I didn't remember seeing any.

"We should close this up until the cops get here," said Charlie.

I looked down at Hanks. He wore an old pair of black loafers that were going to need resoling soon. I wasn't sorry to leave his company. Death is a great measurer. Like it makes the Great Divide look like a foothill by letting you realize how much you liked a person and how much you didn't. I had no use for Hanks but I had never wanted him dead.

Carl and a couple of stable hands were leading Triclops out of the barn. They had covered the horse's eyes with a rag, which didn't make him any happier. On the other hand, he wouldn't be able to see any rats. Frankie Faber and Croteau were standing by the great door. Even standing there, Faber had a beer, which he kept sipping at. Faber was telling Logan where to put the horse, which stall was empty over in the shed row.

At that moment Brenda came tearing into the barn. She pushed through the people like they were so many feather dusters. Her face was all white, even paler than her blond hair. She wore a white blouse and a yellow skirt. Charlie was just shutting the door to the stall. She shoved him aside and yanked it open again. Then she screamed, although "scream" is not really the right word—a sort of shout and a sigh and a great sadness all mixed together. By the time I got to the door, she was down on the straw tugging at Hanks, pulling him around, cradling his head in her arms. "Oh no," she kept saying, "oh no." She was getting blood all over herself. Charlie stood behind her. The professional part of him hated to see her roughhousing the body, the kinder part of him looked sad and patient. She was crying and her face was streaked with tears. I could even see the tears falling onto Hanks's bloody head where they disappeared into his dark hair.

After a few minutes, Charlie touched her shoulder. "The police will be here shortly."

"Leave me alone," she said. "Get out of here."

Charlie moved back a step or two and waited. After another minute, Brenda laid Hanks's body back in the straw, but very gently, as if afraid of waking him up. She got to her feet. The whole front of her white blouse was smeared with blood and there were stains on her yellow skirt. Charlie stood aside to let her leave the stall, then he shut the door behind her.

Out in the feed passage, she wiped the back of her hand across her eyes. The half-dozen stable hands looked at her with horror. She had bloodstains even in her hair. She was dazed and rigid-looking. I had no idea what she might do next, whether she would scream or faint or whatever. She shook her head and glanced around. Croteau and Frankie Faber were still standing by the door. Without a word, Brenda ran at them. She leapt at them and began hitting and clawing at them, kicking them with her boots. Faber's beer went sailing across the floor. It only lasted a moment before Carl grabbed her from behind and held her.

"Help me," he said.

Charlie grabbed her as well. She kept kicking and trying to break free but she didn't make any noise except for grunts. Faber had a long scratch on his cheek and kept rubbing it. His rock-and-roll haircut was all out of shape. Croteau had gotten a kick on the knee and his cowboy hat had fallen off. He was dusting it and looking at Brenda Stanley as if she were some interesting foreign artifact, as if she were not human at all. After another moment she stopped struggling. Then the tears came, great gulping sobs that shook her whole body. Charlie continued to hold on to her. He seemed more distressed by the tears than he had by the kicking and clawing. It was only a few minutes afterward that the state cops began to arrive.

· ● ·

In the next hour or so, all the state cops who had showed up that morning came back again, beginning with Stachek, who looked about as happy as a guy carrying a hundred

pounds of bricks on each of his shoulders up a ladder. I stood
in the parking lot and gave them a big welcome. "Hi, guys.
Long time no see."

Nobody shook my hand or inquired after my health. They
trooped down to the hay barn with their equipment and
scientific paraphernalia. Charlie had taken Brenda back to
her house. She had stopped crying but looked physically
beaten, as if someone had come along and just whacked her
around the chops. She was a pretty woman, but there was
nothing pretty about her face now. Croteau and Frankie Faber
had disappeared somewhere.

I sought out the kid who was supposed to be catching
me the rats. He was in the room that the stable hands used
for a lounge. It wasn't much of a place: a TV, a refrigerator,
a Ping-Pong table, some half-crippled chairs. Some of the
other guys were talking to him, consoling him, trying to make
him forget that he had found a dead man with his head bashed
in. He wasn't about to forget but he appeared to appreciate
the company.

"How'd you happen to find Randall?" I asked him.

The kid blinked at me. His eyes were red and he had a
startled look, not from seeing me but from seeing what life
had dealt him. His reddish-brown hair was mussed. His green
down vest was snapped right up to his neck as if he were
cold.

"I was looking for rats in the hay barn," he said. "Triclops
was banging around in his stall. I had some carrots and I
thought I'd give him one." He dug around in the inside pocket
of his jean jacket and pulled out a dusty carrot. Like it was
proof of his good intentions. "I opened the top half of his
door and saw Mr. Hanks lying in the straw."

"Was Triclops upset?" I asked.

"He was upset but he wasn't, you know, crazy. I mean,
you couldn't blame him for being upset."

"Was there anyone else around?"

"I didn't see anyone."

"What about earlier? Had you seen anyone near the hay barn?"

"No, but I wasn't over there then."

We talked like that for a while. The two other stable hands stood nearby looking glad they hadn't been the ones to find Randall Hanks but also sorry not to be the center of attention.

"What about the rats?" I asked after a while. "How many have you caught?"

"I got nineteen. Will you still give me ten dollars a rat?"

"You bet. Twenty rats, two hundred dollars. But twenty's my limit, don't catch any more than that."

A sergeant showed up to take the kid over to Stachek, who was still in the hay barn. The sergeant wasn't pleased to see me.

"I'm just here muddying the water," I said.

Charlie and I hung around for a couple of hours, like Stachek said we had to stay no matter what. I was afraid that I was going to miss dinner just like I had missed lunch, but then Stachek took my statement around nine-thirty.

"And you're sure you saw nobody near the barn?" he asked. Stachek's brown suit had wisps of straw on the knees. It made him look folksy.

"Not me," I said. "I'd been talking to Carl Logan and had been up in the greenhouse before that. I love flowers."

"What were you talking to Logan about?" We were in the feed passage of the hay barn. A bunch of scientific types were in Triclops's stall. The place was lit up like a movie set. Hanks's body had been already taken away by the ambulance crew.

"You'll have to ask him. I forgot."

"I bet you make trouble for everybody," said Stachek.

He waved his widow's peak at me in a threatening manner. "Not me," I said. "I got a cat who loves me and a granddaughter who's eager to spend the summer with her gramps."

"You ever give anyone a straight answer?" asked Stachek, more curious than rude.

"My doctor says they're bad for my liver," I told him.

A half an hour later I was giving Charlie a ride home in the Mercedes. I felt I'd had a long day and wanted to get a couple of drinks down my gullet so I'd feel half human again. Then I'd have a nice steak sandwich and maybe a little vanilla ice cream. Two corpses in less than a dozen hours made me feel that I was experiencing life more deeply than I cared to experience it.

"So what does Stachek think?" I asked Charlie. "Is poor old Triclops going to get the electric chair?"

"Stachek's pinning his hopes on lab reports," said Charlie. He had rolled back his seat and appeared to be napping. His porkpie hat was tilted over his eyes.

"So he thinks that Triclops might not have killed him?"

"He doesn't know. What's your opinion?"

Up ahead a fat raccoon ambled across my headlights and I slowed down to let it get out of the way. "It seems too tidy," I said. "Like Triclops is solving everybody's problems. Do you think Hanks killed McClintock?"

"I don't know about that either."

"Jesus, Charlie, you're supposed to be the detective. Get on the ball! You got that jury stuff tomorrow?"

Charlie groaned. "That should finish it. They only have one more case."

"Maybe you won't be disqualified."

"I'll lie, cheat and throw a fit in order to be kicked off. What were you doing in the greenhouse?"

"Just sniffing the posies. The gardener says that Logan spent all of his time in there, or at least a whole lot of it."

"Did he grow anything other than orchids?"

"Mostly they're orchids, but he had other tropical plants as well. He had them from all over the world. He was a strange guy. In the past year or so he seems to have given up on the farm almost completely."

"I wish they'd done a complete autopsy," said Charlie.

"Why didn't they?"

"They only wanted to establish cause of death. Since his skull was split open, that didn't take long. And then they looked at his heart as well." Charlie removed his hat and sat up, glanced out the window at the dark fields. "I think I'll learn some more about him," he said.

"Where will you start?"

"I think I'll start with his doctor."

"And what do you want me to do?"

"Logan's got a bunch of horses down at Belmont. Frankie Faber's been working with them. I want to know more about those claiming races. Why don't you drive down to Belmont tomorrow morning and find out about Laurel Hill Farms."

"That's a long way, Charlie."

"Three hours down, three hours back. Good thing you have a nice comfortable car to make the trip."

• ● •

By ten-thirty I was home making myself a stiff Jack Daniel's Manhattan with two maraschino cherries and a dash of bitters. I had been home so infrequently of late that my cat, Moshe III, was pissed off and kept yowling at me from beneath the couch. Sometimes it seems that everybody's got a problem. All this business out at Battlefield Farms had distracted me from my primary concerns, like the stock market could have crashed and I would have known nothing about it. In the mail, I found another missive from my granddaughter Susannah: a short letter talking about her dietary needs and a color snapshot of herself standing next to her rabbi. She was a cute little girl with black braids and I was going to be sorry to disappoint her.

From the car, I had brought up the six copies of the *Saratogian* with Arnette Stroud's scurrilous column on my passion for satanism and child sacrifice. With a pair of scissors I snipped out all six copies and laid them in a row on the kitchen table. Then I sought out six pieces of paper and six envelopes—this took a while because the paper had to be different and the envelopes had to be different, although this difference wasn't so important as with the paper. I found some yellow lined paper and some blank paper and some notebook paper and a postcard showing the Canfield Casino in Congress Park. Then I proceeded to write, I should say create, using my left hand in order to disguise my customary scrawl. Moshe III kept rubbing against my ankles.

"Dear Matthew Plotz: Although we are strangers I feel you should see the enclosed article. It bears strongly on your daughter's summer plans. Your father, Vic, has been talking a lot about human sacrifice. I don't want to butt my nose in where it don't belong, but I think you should think twice before sending your daughter to live with a satanist."

Writing is not easy for me and these letters took a while. I was on my third Jack Daniel's Manhattan before I was done.

"Dear Matt Plotz: Consider me an unknown friend. You must be out of your effing gourd to send your sweet daughter into such a hellhole as I know your old man's den of iniquity to be. Even though he is luring her for all he is worth, I would bite the bullet and keep her at home, otherwise she is bound to come to a bad end. Please read the enclosed article. Believe me, satanism is only the beginning."

There must have been something about my leaving New York City back in the seventies, like I must have been really sick of it, because by the time I reached the Tappan Zee Bridge around seven-thirty Wednesday morning my stomach had started cramping up and my palms were as damp as a bad baby's butt. Usually the Mercedes is an easy drive but I was crouched over the steering wheel, hanging on with both fists. The turnpike was already packed with cars seeing how fast they could hustle and it felt like my biological clock was telling me it was time to spawn. Once I got onto Long Island, however, and was headed away from Manhattan, the driving got easier. Despite the potholes and broken glass, fewer cars tried to sideswipe me and no one gave me the finger. The sky was a gray drizzle, one of those spring days when winter is trying to make a return engagement and is failing badly, which turns it sullen and spiteful. The trees were already in full leaf, like the city was about two weeks ahead of Saratoga, weatherwise. Around eight-thirty I parked in the big empty lot at Belmont, then headed for the backstretch. Through the fence I could see horses with mellow question-mark expressions walking to and from the track to be exercised.

The stands at Belmont are not as pretty as the stands at

Saratoga but they are bigger and more dramatic. The backstretch, however, looks about the same, with big trees, and horses being walked here and there, and lots of roosters and goats and dogs which are kept around because they make the horses feel relaxed. Can you imagine the psychology of an animal that it takes a goat to relax? The pace of any backstretch is exaggeratedly unhasty and the only people in a rush are the jockey's agents as they make their rounds trying to pick up mounts for their guys. In fact, the big rule of the backstretch is No Running. The horses must be made to think that it is a drowsy world out there, full of happy, slow-moving people. Private cops cool their heels at the intersections between the shed rows, and when the exercise riders come up behind you, they whisper, "Watch your back." I guess all this is meant to fool the horses that life's single frantic event is that hysterical minute or two of the race, after which everyone returns to napping and eating. It doesn't seem like a bad philosophy as far as philosophies go.

Battlefield Farms had a barn near the little lunch counter in the middle of the backstretch. Horses were still being exercised so there was a lot of movement, like each one of these horses has an agenda. If he is not being raced today, then it is tomorrow or the day after, and his feed and exercise and vitamins and his jolly leg rub all depend on that agenda, meaning when he is being raced and is he coming into form and how his psychic life is doing and does his shit look happy. Personally speaking, I'm a fast-moving fellow and I probably have more in common with the jockeys' agents than with anyone else in the backstretch, but there is something so peaceful about the place that visiting it, I often think I could be perfectly happy walking a horse in a circle for the rest of my life, that's how crazy I become.

The barn being used by Battlefield Farms was being run by an assistant trainer in Frankie Faber's absence. This was an older guy from Kentucky named Moses Wilcox. At first I thought he might be Jewish because of his first name, but he looked like a regular Wasp so I figured Moses was just a common name back in Kentucky in the 1930s or whenever his folks decided to burden him with it. Moses wore old khaki pants and a khaki shirt. He was a soft-looking guy, going bald, with a tanned face from being outside a lot, and wire granny glasses. He was suspicious of me, but he was also desperate to know what was happening at Battlefield Farms, like he knew that Logan had been buried the day before, and that McClintock and Hanks had been found dead within twelve hours of each other. It seemed that the organization that employed him was self-destructing, which resulted in the situation where he wanted to ask questions but was leery about answering them.

"How long have you worked for Battlefield Farms?" I asked. We were in an office in a corner of the barn which had whitewashed wooden walls and a bunch of bridles and stuff hanging from hooks. Wilcox stood behind the desk. He seemed too nervous to sit down and relax.

"About a year," he said. "Faber hired me. Look, do you have some identification other than that badge?"

"I must have left it in my car," I said. "Feel free to give Carl Logan a call, if you want." I put the little brass badge that said "Detective" back in my pocket.

"And you're a private detective?"

"Bradshaw Enterprises."

"What does Logan want with a private detective?" His tone suggested that the only thing one could want with a private detective was general nastiness, like blackmail or bullying.

"He wants to make sure that no one is cheating him. Also his dad got murdered, McClintock was shot and Hanks got himself kicked to death. It's a jumpy place up there. Lots of people are spending lots of time looking over their shoulders. So you see yourself as working primarily for Croteau?"

Wilcox ignored my question. "But Hanks wasn't murdered, right? It was just an accident."

"The cops haven't decided yet. You have an alibi?"

Wilcox got angry. It made his forehead all wrinkled. "I been down here two weeks, ask anybody. What the hell you suggesting I need an alibi for?"

"So you see your loyalties as belonging to Croteau, rather than Logan?"

"I work for Faber. Faber tells me what to do."

"Tell me something," I said, rubbing the palms of my hands together. "Faber's been losing some pretty good horses in claiming races. You know anything about that?"

Wilcox leaned forward over the desk, supporting himself on his arms. He looked like he wanted to shout but was thinking better of it. "Everybody loses horses. You got a problem with it, then talk to Faber." Wilcox stared down at the desk for a moment, then asked, "Did McClintock shoot himself?"

"He may have had some help. The gun wasn't pressed up against his head. He was assistant trainer, right? Just like you. By the way, what do you know about Laurel Hill Farms?"

Wilcox got angry again and his face got red like a sunset. It was pretty but not worth a picture. Sometimes I worry about the amount of stress I put on other guys' hearts.

"I can't spend all morning answering your questions," Wilcox said in a moderate bellow. "You know I got horses to run today? You have a question, then ask Faber. Not me. And if it's me that you want, then you'll have to talk to my lawyer."

"Are you always so touchy," I asked, "or are you getting your period? Male PMS is a scary business."

"You know I could have you thrown out of here?" He took two steps around the desk as if wondering whether he could heave me out on his own. I don't heave easy. He stopped and faced me with his hands pressed flat to his sides.

I gave him a hearty smile. "If you so much as touch me, you'll have to dig yourself out from under a lawsuit like south Florida had to dig itself out of Hurricane Andrew. So tell me again about Laurel Hill Farms."

But Moses Wilcox wasn't having any. I could talk to Faber or I could talk to Wilcox's lawyer, but Wilcox himself was the living statue of silence incarnate.

"So you have no idea who might have killed Neil McClintock?"

"Get out!" he shouted.

Well, he was almost silence incarnate.

Leaving the barn, I strolled over to the steward's office. It seemed that somebody had to know about Laurel Hill Farms and the steward's office was my best bet. The drizzle had stopped and a little sun was peeking through the trees. A rooster was crowing and I liked the note of optimism in its voice.

· ● ·

Two hours later, I was recrossing the Tappan Zee Bridge heading north. Not only was I cheery, but the Mercedes was positively bouncing from pothole to pothole. It was nice to be heading north rather than south. The steward's office had not exactly welcomed me with open arms, but from a functionary in a blue suit I had learned several pieces of hot information. One, Laurel Hill Farms was the stable that had claimed the three horses away from Frankie Faber. Two, Laurel Hill Farms was not assigned any stall space in the backstretch, meaning the horses were not being raced at Belmont. Three, the only address for Laurel Hill Farms was a post office box in Kingston. Four, Laurel Hill Farms had only been registered with the racing association for about six months.

The big question was why Croteau had a file on Laurel Hill Farms in his file cabinet and one far larger than he needed were he simply noting that the farm had claimed three of his stepfather's horses. I was sorry I hadn't swiped the file, and once again it reminded me that half measures were bad measures. If you are going to be crooked, then you got to be crooked all the way.

By one-thirty I was back in dear old Saratoga, and my first stop was my duplex to turn up the pressure on Ernie Flako. His Harley was parked at the curb and there was a little scratch on the front fender from where it had gotten accidentally tipped over on Monday.

Puma answered the door. She was wearing a kind of pink sarong and a bikini top which displayed the jungle tattoos on her large breasts to full advantage. Her thick black hair obscured half her face and fell over her shoulders. The pit bull was barking in the background.

"You know," I told her, "if instead of jungle tattoos you had equations and mathematical theorems, then I could admire your beauty and intelligence at exactly the same time."

"Ernie!" shouted Puma. "The creep's here again!"

"Are those monkeys swinging on their vines," I asked, "or are they small pictures of your beloved?"

"You're disgusting," she said and crossed her arms over her breasts.

"Why'd you get those tattoos if you don't want them looked at?"

"There're not for you to look at. They're only for special people to look at." Puma swirled her black hair and curled her full lips into a scornful expression. I could have swapped wisecracks with her all day long.

"Next time I'll shut my eyes," I said.

But then Ernie was at the door, shoving Puma aside. "You knocked over my machine, man."

"Do you have a witness?"

"I don't need a witness."

"For the court you need a witness, but before God maybe you don't. Do you have my money?"

"What I owe you is what it will cost to fix that scratch."

"Nine hundred bucks?"

"It's precision work." Ernie grinned. He was missing some teeth. He wore a gray undershirt and jeans. Thick black hair poked through the cracks of the undershirt. Puma looked at him proudly. She thought he looked primal; I thought he looked rudimentary.

"Look, Ernie, I'm afraid you have to get out of here. Move, vacate, transport yourself. Otherwise I will make you. It could be painful, it could be traumatic. I'd hate to see you hurt."

"Yeah," said Ernie, getting truculent and showing me one of his biceps, "you and who else?"

This seemed to be his standard answer. "Me and a bunch of little pals," I said.

"That'll be the day," said Ernie.

Chitchat with Ernie wasn't as fun as chitchat with his helpmate, so I walked back to my Mercedes. Ernie followed to make sure that nothing happened to his Harley. But I had bigger plans than putting a few scratches on his bike. The Harley had become small potatoes. Nor was I disappointed with my lack of success. I had foreseen Ernie's response to my polite request, but it was necessary to give him the chance. I had said to Ernie: Two paths lie before you—the path of virtue and the path of terrible trouble. I had to let Ernie choose his own course in order to make him responsible for whatever happened next.

• ● •

Around three o'clock I was sitting at my kitchen table studying what the stock market had been up to since I had last pressed my finger to its erratic pulse and mopping up the remains of a Reuben sandwich when the buzzer gave its little howl of protest to indicate that a potential visitor was dawdling downstairs. I called down to see who it was and soon Eddie Gillespie was hammering on my door, breathless with excitement. He wore a tan suit with some muddy smudges on the pants and jacket. He carried a plastic bag with something heavy inside.

"I got this case cracked wide open," he said, hurrying through the door.

Eddie, when he is playing private detective, likes to be competitive with me. He was expecting me to die of curiosity and whine jealously about his successes. Instead, I yawned. After all, I had hit the road to Belmont around five-thirty.

"Don't you care?" Eddie persisted.

"Sure I care, Eddie, but a case like this has lots of complicated angles which would be lost on you. I mean, Charlie's dealing with Einstein's Theory of Relativity and you're back practicing your times tables. You got to stop reading about Dick and Jane, Eddie, this is *War and Peace*."

"I drove by Charlie's place but he wasn't there," said Eddie, ignoring my metaphoric folderol. "So I figured I'd stop by here. Come on, Vic, this is important stuff!"

"Okay, Eddie, what d'you got?"

Eddie opened his plastic bag above my kitchen table. I should say that I had a lot of important and very neat papers carefully stacked in four different piles depending on the quality of their stock market activity during the week. When Eddie opened the plastic bag, a couple of pounds of horseshit rained down on top of them. This was followed by a baseball bat, which crashed down hard. But it wasn't your run-of-the-mill Louisville Slugger. It was a baseball bat with a horseshoe screwed onto the end of it.

"Nice," I said. "Where did you get it?" I picked it up, admiring its heft.

Eddie patted himself on the chest. His shiny hair bounced up, then collapsed into a new and luxurious configuration of dark ringlets. "I was out at the farm around lunchtime and I saw this Frankie Faber guy sneaking out of the horse barn carrying this garbage bag. He looked suspicious so I followed him. He went around to the back where all this manure was shoveled and he buried this in it. Then, when he went away, I went and got it."

"Did you consider calling the cops?" I asked.

"Nah, why bother?"

"And you touched it, maybe? You swung it around a few times?"

"Sure. I mean, I wanted to see how it worked."

I too had touched it. I took out a Kleenex and tried to wipe around the handle, then I gave it up. "Do you know what Lieutenant Stachek is going to say to us?"

Eddie looked at me hopefully. " 'Thanks'?"

"No, Eddie, he's going to say, 'You fuckin dumbo, you been tampering with evidence.' You know the charges he can press? The fines you would have to pay? Even jail, Eddie, he can throw your ass in jail."

Eddie looked at the baseball bat rather thoughtfully. "Maybe we should just throw the fucker away."

"What do you mean 'we,' kemosabe?"

"You think I could just put it back?"

"And what about the fingerprints? If we rub off ours, then

we rub off Faber's as well. Then who's to say that Faber was actually the one to bury it? It's your word against his."

"Damn," said Eddie. "I'm sorry I ever found the darn thing."

"Don't take it so hard, Eddie. I'll drive the bat over to Charlie's a little later. Maybe he'll have an idea. And at least you were keeping your eyes peeled, right? That's half of the detective's job."

"What's the other half? Being tough?"

"No, Eddie. Thinking."

Well, you might assume I was planning to take the bat over to Charlie's and claim credit for its discovery, but I knew that bringing it away from the farm was a mistake and that I would get yelled at just as Eddie would get yelled at. Eddie had gone to my refrigerator and gotten himself a Beck's. Now he was sitting at my kitchen table, sipping his beer and fiddling with a little chunk of horseshit that had fallen out of the plastic bag. I removed my papers, first wiping them off.

"By the way, Eddie, how would you like to move into a new place? Clean, well lit and within walking distance of Saratoga's major downtown attractions."

"You mean one of your dumps?"

"Not dumps, Eddie. It hurts me to hear you call them dumps. These are fine duplexes with backyards suitable for the frolic and play of a child of your child's tender years. A duplex, Eddie—didn't you say you needed a place for your mother-in-law right nearby for baby-sitting purposes?"

"What about the biker?" asked Eddie.

I had told Eddie nothing about the biker so I assumed that Charlie had been talking.

"He'll be out of there by this weekend."

"How do you know?"

"I know, that's all." I got myself a Beck's from the refrigerator and sat down at the kitchen table across from Eddie. The horseshoe was screwed sideways onto the end of the bat. It looked like a home run right into poor Randall Hanks's brains, what few there had been.

"And this is a twelve-month lease?"

"Ten and a half. You'd have to vacate in mid-July but you could come back on September first."

"So what would we do during that time?"

"You could go camping. It's fun, Eddie. Take the whole family, rediscover America's roots in a tepee."

"For six weeks?"

"It would be a learning experience. You owe it to your daughter."

"Six weeks in a tepee with my mother-in-law?"

"You'd grow close."

"We'd kill each other."

It seemed that Eddie always had a complaint, that whatever he was offered was never good enough. "Why is it, Eddie, that you always disappoint me?"

"Because you never offer me anything but shit, that's why. Look, you can move into the tepee for six weeks and we'll take over your apartment. How does that sound?"

"I'd be happy to, Eddie, but my lumbago would be the death of me. Hard ground, damp air—it's a young person's pleasure and an old person's curse. It would make a man of you and a corpse of me."

"Maybe your granddaughter would like the tepee." Then he made a woof-woof noise like a half-suppressed laugh. "And when she gets here, you'll have to take down these ugly pictures."

Eddie was remarking on the nude photographs of the Queen of Softness.

"Who's this old bag anyhow?" he asked.

"My paramour, the woman who accentuates the beating of my pulse."

"She looks like a candidate for Weight Watchers to me. Look at that skin, that flab, those sagging chunks of flesh!"

"You're privileging outdated stereotypes of beauty, Eddie. She's the butter I spread across the hot toast of my body, the marshmallow sauce into which I dunk my personal ice cream."

"From what I can see," said Eddie, "she's pure cholesterol." Then he turned away.

· ● ·

Charlie was no more pleased with Eddie's swiping the baseball bat with the horseshoe screwed to the end than I had been.

"You should have left it there," he said sadly.

"But I didn't know what he was burying until I dug it out," said Eddie.

"Then you should have put it back and called the police."

Charlie had gotten home early and Eddie and I had driven out to his place around four-thirty. Charlie had been kicked off the jury panel. Maybe "disqualified" is the word. "It was a dog-bite case," Charlie had said. "I told the defense lawyer that I was an ex-policeman and a full-time private detective and that I could read the evidence professionally and that his client deserved to be sent away for at least ten years. I didn't mince my words. I just wanted to get out of there. So the judge asked why I hadn't announced at the beginning that I was a former policeman and I said I hadn't thought it was important and he said I probably could have gotten disqualified on the first day, and that didn't surprise me any. I mean, I wasn't surprised that I had made that kind of mistake."

And I thought that was typical of Charlie, like he slogs

through life like a guy might slog through a swimming pool full of raspberry Jell-O, and only after he has gone the full length of the pool does he learn that he could have taken the shortcut around the side. So he was not in the best of moods and when we showed up with the baseball bat and he learned what Eddie had done, Charlie jumped all over him.

"You'll be lucky if Stachek doesn't put you in jail," said Charlie. When Charlie gets mad, he lowers his voice instead of raises it. He spoke to Eddie in a whisper.

"Even though I got a wife and kid?" asked Eddie.

"Jesse James had a wife and *two* kids," said Charlie, "and it didn't help him any."

But at last Charlie decided we should drive out to Battlefield Farms and confront Faber with the baseball bat. Maybe we could get a confession out of him. Charlie had gingerly taken the bat out of the bag and inspected it. Maybe there were bloodstains on the horseshoe, but maybe not. From having bounced around in horseshit all afternoon, it was hard to tell what were bloodstains and what were horseshit stains.

"At least it looks like Triclops won't get the chair," I said. "Poor horse got framed."

As we drove out Battlefield Road, I told Charlie about my trip to Belmont and what I had learned about Laurel Hill Farms.

"Did you get the names of the people who run it?" asked Charlie.

"There was only that post office box in Kingston."

"But if it's a registered corporation, then it must have a board of directors and a chairman. That's all right, I'll check it out in the morning."

"What about Randall Hanks?" I asked. "Did you ask Stachek about him?"

"He says that the lab told him that Hanks had possibly been killed by Triclops or possibly not."

"What's that supposed to mean?"

"The indentation in Hanks's skull came from one of Triclops's shoes, but there was no other matter: no hoof matter or hair. Also there didn't seem to be sufficient blood on the straw around the body, meaning he might have been killed someplace else and then dumped in the stall."

"So he might possibly have been killed by a baseball bat with a horseshoe attached," I said.

"Sure he was," said Eddie Gillespie from the backseat. "What's all this possibly-possibly stuff?"

"We're professionals," I said. "This is how professionals talk."

"Sounds fuckin wishy-washy to me," said Eddie.

In the rearview mirror, I watched him toss his ornamental hair. I couldn't wait until he went bald.

·   ●   ·

We caught up with Frankie Faber as he was walking across the yard from the training track to the horse barn. He was as happy to see us as he would have been to see a case of cholera. He was wearing jeans and a green workshirt and dangling from his left hand was a bottle of Budweiser, like I don't think I had ever seen him without a beer. His memorial statue might have been called *The Eternal Sipper*. Eddie had gone off on some pseudo-detective errands so Charlie and I were with Faber by ourselves. Not many other people were around and I later learned that some of the stable hands had been laid off. It's hard to run an active stable when people keep getting murdered.

"Hey," I said to Frankie, "how's the racing biz?"

Charlie nudged me aside. "I wonder if we might talk to you for a moment, Mr. Faber."

Frankie gave us a look that was shy on warm feeling.

Even his rock-and-roll haircut appeared flatter. "What about?" he asked.

"Well, we're very concerned about what had been happening here," said Charlie, as mild as milk.

"You think I'm not?" asked Faber, his voice rising. Then he stopped himself and took another pull on his beer.

Charlie put a hand on Frankie's shoulder and began walking him toward his office. He was taller than Frankie by about three inches, which he must have liked because usually Charlie isn't taller than anybody. The late-afternoon sun shimmered on the white buildings.

"What do you know about Laurel Hill Farms?" asked Charlie.

Frankie stiffened as sharply as if someone's icy fingers had just slapped him a dose of Preparation H. "I don't think I recognize the name."

"Sure you do," said Charlie. "That's the outfit that claimed those three horses."

"Oh yeah," said Frankie, suddenly remembering. "They pulled quite a coup."

"Some people think you gave them the horses on purpose," said Charlie.

"How dare you say that!" Frankie made a little hop. Small and nervous, he resembled a little rooster.

By now we had reached his office. I opened the door and waited for them to enter. I was carrying the baseball bat, which we had wrapped up in newspaper. Frankie glanced at it nervously, both wondering what it might be and afraid of what it might be.

"I'm not suggesting anything," said Charlie. "I'm just telling you what other people have said."

"What other people?"

"People who have since died."

The screen door swung shut with a bang and Frankie

jumped. "Are you saying I had anything to do with that?" He stood by his desk. He looked angry and frightened by turns, like a light which first flicked one color, then another. The office had been cleaned up since McClintock's death the previous morning but I bet that if I searched hard, I could still find a smidgen of his gore. If I had been Frankie, I would have chosen to work someplace else.

"Say, Frankie," I asked, "who are those people who run Laurel Hill Farms?"

Frankie sipped his beer. "I know nothing about it."

"It seems to be a new outfit down around Kingston," said Charlie. "You mean you never looked into who was claiming your horses, your very best horses?"

"I had other things to do." Frankie's face had gotten all tight. His back was to the wall but he still didn't intend to confide in us. He was the opposite of Pavarotti: small and silent.

"Come on, Frankie," I said. "You're being less than truthful with your pals. Here's a brand-new organization scoring off you—d'you mean you never looked into it?"

"I'm just the trainer," said Frankie with sudden modesty. "You got other questions, then go to Mr. Croteau."

"Could he tell us about Laurel Hill Farms?" I asked.

Frankie drank some more beer. "I'm not saying yes, I'm not saying no."

"Let's call him right now," said Charlie. "Is he over at his house?"

"No," said Frankie, looking relieved, "he had to go into Saratoga."

"How convenient," said Charlie. He took off his porkpie hat, blew into it, then put it back on his head.

"Tell me, Frankie," I said, "what did you have against Randall Hanks?"

"What d'you mean?"

"You know, likes and dislikes. Some people we cotton to, some people we hate. Did Hanks know about this scam you were pulling with Laurel Hill Farms?"

"Dammit, there was no scam!" shouted Frankie. His eyes got all whirly, as if he were trying to swallow his panic but it had gotten stuck someplace behind his windpipe.

"Then what did you have against Hanks?" asked Charlie.

"Except that he was fuckin the boss's wife, I had nothing against him." Frankie finished his beer and looked at the bottle sadly, as if bidding goodbye to an old pal. There was a small refrigerator against the wall with a beer case on top. Frankie put the empty into the beer case and opened the refrigerator. "Dammit to hell!" he shouted. "People are always stealing my beer. There was a whole six-pack in here earlier today."

Over Frankie's shoulder I could see one lone bottle of Bud. Frankie snatched for it, in case I might ask for a little. He was not a guy who liked to share.

When Frankie had his back to us, I took the baseball bat out of its newspaper wrapping. When Frankie turned around with his bottle of beer, I was holding it out to him.

"Hey, Frankie," I said, "Lieutenant Stachek wants to know why you were burying this club this morning."

If Frankie had had false teeth, he would have swallowed them. His whole body clapped to attention, and through the thin transparency of his forehead it seemed I could see the sentence "The jig's up!" pass across his brain. He twisted off the top of the Budweiser but he was too startled to drink.

"Just hiding that bat could put you in jail for a long time," said Charlie conversationally.

"Two murders," I said, "or is it three?"

Frankie started talking fast. "It was in my room. Somebody stuck it there. What am I supposed to do, call the cops? Somebody was trying to frame me." He paused to take a drink of beer. "As for Laurel Hill Farms, you can ask Croteau about that. I told him not to do it. Three horses, he was bound to get caught. He was even planning a fourth." He took another drink, then stared at the bottle as if it had let him down in some deep and nefarious manner. "But it wasn't like he was really being crooked. . . ."

Frankie's voice had changed slightly and became raspy. He took a smaller sip of beer, then looked wonderingly at the bottle. "Somebody's been fuckin with this," he said. "That goddam. . . ."

And that was it. Faber began breathing rapidly and gasping for breath. He dropped the bottle, which didn't break but went rolling. Holding on to his stomach, he staggered back toward his desk, then he began throwing up across it, nasty heaving retching sounds. Charlie and I watched, both of us surprised. Faber turned toward us again, his jaw and shirt wet with beer vomit. He opened his mouth to speak, then his knees gave way and he fell to the floor.

10

Frankie Faber managed to hang on to this world for four more hours but I didn't see him again and he didn't talk. An ambulance got him over to the hospital in Saratoga, but all of it took a while. Frankie's stomach was pumped and the doctors decided it was cyanide poisoning. They gave him amyl nitrite, sodium nitrite and sodium thiosulfate, but it all came too late for Frankie and he went up to meet the angels. The cops of course wanted to know where the cyanide had come from, but the answer was easy. All week long people had been buying rat poison like crazy, and the biggest purchase had been made by Randall Hanks on Monday.

I was beginning to feel sorry for Lieutenant Stachek and his team of eager beavers. They trooped back with their lights, bags of equipment and heavy expressions. Stachek couldn't even manage a friendly hello and snarled when he saw me. I had picked up Frankie's spilled bottle of beer—like it was an important clue, right?—and Stachek acted as if I had been messing with important evidence. Now my fingerprints were mixed up with the others. All I did was make more work for the cops, et cetera, et cetera. As for the baseball bat with the horseshoe attached, I thought Stachek was going to throw

Eddie Gillespie and me in a dungeon and then weld the door shut so it could never be opened again.

"You did what?" he kept saying. "You did what?"

Stachek seemed to feel that Eddie and I had been put on this earth to make him as miserable as a monogamous monkey, and when I told him I had a life full of important business that had nothing to do with him and began to talk about the Queen of Softness and the beauty of older women, I thought Lieutenant Stachek was going to go up like a firecracker.

"You know that man might have been saved," shouted Stachek, "if you had told us about that baseball bat right away?"

Stachek wore a dark gray suit which matched the dark stubble shadows on his face. His black widow's peak looked positively lethal. I decided that silence was my wisest course and I put my hands behind my back and stared at the floor.

"You as good as poisoned him yourself!" he shouted.

We were in Faber's office, and even the lab crew seemed nervous of Stachek. I tried to give one of the shorter scientists a comradely wink but he ignored me.

"You know how many years you could spend behind bars?" Stachek shouted.

Well, Charlie had to do a lot of soothing and placating, and I felt that even Charlie was losing his luster as far as Stachek was concerned. Stachek had been out at the farm for several hours during the day and had talked to everybody and had made everybody uncomfortable, but he hadn't learned anything. Or rather, he had learned lots of stuff but nothing he could slap somebody into the slammer for. As for the poisoned bottle of Budweiser, anybody could have opened it, filled it with nasty juice and recapped it. Anybody could have slipped into Faber's office, swiped the rest of the beer and left this one tainted bottle. There were still ten stable hands or workers or grooms or whatever wandering around, plus Carl Logan, Brenda Stanley and Donald Croteau. And other people had shown up during the day: a trainer from another farm, a tack salesman, feed guys, the vet. Lieutenant Stachek's list of who had opportunity was like the Mississippi River: long and muddy.

It was my position that if Stachek was truly on the ball, then he would have solved the case by now, but Charlie persuaded me to keep this idea to myself. After telling Stachek most of what we knew and being yelled at until the lieutenant had nearly lost his voice and was croaking like a frog, he kicked us out of the office and told us to wait outside.

As I was leaving, I said, "Hey, Stachek, how are you and Triclops the same?"

Charlie, behind me, gave me a rude push into the open air and shut the door.

"I was going to tell him they were both a little hoarse," I said, aggrieved.

"I know what you were going to tell him," said Charlie. He sounded like he had had it up to the portholes with his pal.

We stood around cooling our heels. Donald Croteau came back from Saratoga and one of the cops took him over to Stachek. I would have liked to talk to him first, but that was not allowed. I felt like a chiropractor being sneered at by a bunch of snobby M.D.s. Croteau looked stunned, which I thought was pretty good for someone who usually showed no facial expression. The ruddy skin of his face seemed stretched as tight as the skin on a snare drum. Even his freckles looked paler. He saw us but gave no expression of recognition, like he didn't so much see us as wipe his eyes across us.

Charlie was talking to Carl Logan, who had walked across the yard to join us. It was getting dark and the bats were again scarfing up the bugs. Logan, too, seemed stunned.

He kept shaking his head and pushing his hands through his hair. All these guys had had a life which they had figured was going in a straight line, despite the bumps and bruises, and here it had made a radical turn to the left and was behaving like a roller coaster or like Triclops when he met the rat. They all had the sense there was something unfair about it, as if life was supposed to behave itself and stay on course and be nice to everybody. Like that's what I had thought when my wife died: that it wasn't fair, that life wasn't behaving properly. Since then, I don't believe in fairness. I only believe in jokes, but maybe that's not entirely true, because I also hoped that whoever was causing all this trouble at Battlefield Farms would be packed away to Auburn almost forever. Four corpses constituted an epidemic.

While we were standing around and nighttime was replacing daytime, we were joined by the kid who was catching me the rats.

"I got all twenty," he told me. Like he was proud the way Van Cliburn was proud when he won the Russian competition.

"You got them in a cage?" I asked.

"Sure."

"You keeping them fed and happy?"

"Fed at least," said the kid.

"I'll pick them up tomorrow morning," I told him. "No later than nine o'clock. Two hundred bucks, just like I said."

After the kid had strolled away again, Charlie tapped me on the shoulder. "May I ask you a personal question?" he said.

"Shoot."

"What do you plan to do with twenty rats?"

"It's personal, Charlie. You'd be better off not knowing."

Charlie appeared to think about this, then he said, "Do you have any idea of how close you are to jail? Stachek would give a week's vacation for the opportunity to lock you up."

I put a finger to my lips. "Then we better not tell him,"
I said.

• ● •

Around nine-thirty that Wednesday night, Charlie and I
walked over to Croteau's small ranch house for a chat. Stachek had done talking to him, had done talking to everybody,
and the cops were just finishing up. By that time Frankie
Faber had been dead about half an hour. The hospital had
called and Stachek passed the news along. He didn't speak
to me, he only glared. I had the sense that if he had spoken
to me, he would have started screaming. Like his antipathy
was almost a chemical thing. He looked at me and shivered.
I gave him a smile just to show I bore no hard feelings and
he stamped away.

Croteau didn't seem particularly glad to see us. If his face
had seemed tight before, now it was a little tighter. He took
us into his living room. Like I said, the motel-modern furniture was covered with plastic which made it slippery and
unpleasant to the touch. The room had pale yellow walls and
no pictures, only a mirror over the couch. Charlie and I sat
on the couch; Croteau sat in an uncomfortable-looking armchair. He resembled a machine that had just been switched
on and was now warming up. He wore khaki pants, a blue
plaid shirt and a gray tweed jacket. His light brown hair was
perfectly combed. Even his freckles looked neat and in a row.
I would have liked to have known about his sex life. I mean,
it was one of those questions which I wanted to ask and
which I felt might give me a handle on him. It wasn't that he
seemed gay or heterosexual or asexual; it was just that I could
get no reading at all. He was as self-contained as a block of
wood and twice as private.

Charlie put on his expression which said that he was a

serious and deeply feeling human being who was just trying
to figure out the world's mysterious complications which were
almost proving too much for him. He was leaning forward
with his elbows on his knees. He held his porkpie hat with
both hands and was turning it round and round by the brim
so that it looked like a motor idling. His bifocals glittered.
Then he sighed.

"I'm having trouble with this Laurel Hill Farms," said
Charlie. "It seems to be a new place and its only purpose
seems to have been to claim horses away from your stepfather,
the very best horses. Three horses got claimed and from what
Frankie Faber said you were planning to lose a fourth. What
I'm saying is, you must be Laurel Hill Farms yourself."

Well, I made a little jump on the couch and if Croteau
hadn't been staring at us, I would have patted Charlie's head.

"Go on," said Croteau. "Let's see you work out your
little theory."

"You own forty percent of Battlefield Farms," said Charlie. "Your stepfather wanted to buy you out, but you wouldn't
sell. You knew he wanted to turn his part of the farm over
to Carl and you didn't want that. But you'd no sense that
Carl had any interest in the farm until he came back from
college last year. His return changed the balance of power.
You didn't want Carl to have the farm and you no longer
wanted to stay yourself, so you formed another corporation—Laurel Hill Farms—and began claiming away your
stepfather's best stock, that is, seemed to claim the horses
away from yourself. Most likely you planned to claim some
more horses and then offer to sell out, forcing your stepfather
to buy something which, while certainly not worthless, you
had severely weakened. His death put a stop to that because
it again changed the terms, the balance of power."

"So you don't think I killed him?"

"You might have. If he'd discovered how you and Faber

were claiming the horses away from the farm, he could have pressed charges. Conspiracy to defraud would put a severe crimp in your style. You might have killed him to keep that from happening."

Croteau sat with his hands in his lap. He seemed never to move, never to blink. "Have you told Stachek about this?"

"Not yet."

"I still didn't kill him," said Croteau. "But you're right about Laurel Hill Farms. I wanted to wreck him. He wanted to give the farm to Carl and I wanted to turn it into a shambles. I knew he was bound to work out some deal with Brenda for her part of the farm and that would give Carl sixty percent. I would have been no more than a flunky. So I started a new farm. I got Faber to enter those horses in cheap claiming races and then claimed them myself. I can't tell you how good it felt."

When Croteau said this, he blinked his eyes. He blinked them once. It was like seeing one of those big guys on Mount Rushmore blink.

"Let's say, just for the sake of speculation," said Charlie, "that you didn't kill your stepfather. What about the others?"

"I figure Randall killed McClintock," said Croteau. "He thought that McClintock had put the rat cage over Triclops's stall and was trying to frame him."

"And who killed Hanks?" asked Charlie.

"Your guy saw Faber burying that club," said Croteau. "Faber must have killed him. After all, McClintock was found dead on Frankie's desk. If it wasn't suicide, then somebody was trying to frame Frankie."

"And who poisoned Frankie?" asked Charlie.

"Hanks was the one who bought rat poison," said Croteau. "He could have put the poison into those bottles before he was killed and left them in Frankie's refrigerator. As a matter of fact, Frankie had a couple of refrigerators. I told that to the lieutenant and he sent one of his men to check the others. I don't know what they found."

"So it's all over," said Charlie. "The killers have managed to kill each other. Is that right?"

Croteau gave an infinitesimal smile. "That's what I think," he said.

"And what about the conspiracy-to-defraud charge?"

"My stepfather's no longer around to press charges. I now own the biggest portion of the farm, so I'll get those horses back again. I'll do whatever I'm forced to do. I guess you'll be telling Brenda and Carl about Laurel Hill Farms?"

"I guess," said Charlie.

Half an hour later, I was giving Charlie a ride back to his place on the lake. Eddie Gillespie was snoozing in the back seat.

"So nothing can be done against Croteau," I said.

"I don't know. Maybe Carl or Brenda Stanley can sue him, but he can always return the horses and probably will."

"So what d'you think?" I asked.

"I think Croteau thinks it's over, but it's not over," said Charlie.

"I think Yogi Berra said it better," I said.

And from the backseat the sleepy voice of Goofy Gillespie lumbered toward the obvious: "It's not over till it's finished, or something like that."

• ● •

The next morning I drove back out to Battlefield Farms to pick up my rats. A guy can make a pack of trouble with twenty rats and I had a lot of chuckles about all the trouble I could generate, like I would be the Grand Coulee Dam of trouble. It was raining hard and my windshield wipers were going whap-whap. It was one of those solid business rains you get in the spring and you could almost feel the flowers stretching out their little necks to grope the drops. The fields were a gray mist and the horizon seemed only a stone's throw away.

I felt drowsily relaxed. I'd visited the Queen of Softness the previous night and we had spent several hours playing footsy in her hot tub, which had made our skin so wrinkled and accordionesque that we had to massage each other with baby oil just to regain our luster. Afterward we cooked steaks and knocked off a bottle of Beaujolais. I told her about Battlefield Farms and how I figured out that criminal mischief of Donald Croteau's with him swiping his own horses, or the farm's horses, and how Frankie Faber had died at my feet. In my stories to her I make myself a little bigger and she treats me a little kinder. But I didn't tell her about how I had sent those newspaper articles about my supposed satanism to my son, nor did I tell her about my plans with the rats. The Queen of Softness has a sweet streak—I wouldn't have it any other way—and she disapproves of some of my peppy pranks.

When I pulled into the parking lot by the greenhouse, I saw that no horses were being exercised out on the training track. Maybe it was because of the rain, but I didn't think so. More likely the horse-racing activities of Battlefield Farms were being put on hold for a while. In fact, down by the shed row a horse was being coaxed into a trailer and I would not have been surprised if some of the owners who had signed their nags up with Battlefield Farms had decided to move their equine equity someplace else for a while: someplace where murders didn't occur and horses were regularly run.

Next to my Mercedes in the parking lot was Eddie Gillespie's red pickup truck with the chrome pipes. I was not pleased to see it. If Lieutenant Stachek could accuse me of muddying the water, I could also accuse Eddie of muddying the water. As I turned away, I saw a little flash from the greenhouse and I headed over in that direction, pulling up the collar of my raincoat and pulling down my Gore-Tex golfing cap.

Eddie Gillespie was in the greenhouse taking pictures of the flowers with a Polaroid camera. Seeing him, I was certain he had lost his marbles; or rather, he had not simply lost his marbles, he had ripped them from his head and thrown them to the wind.

When Eddie noticed me, he nodded briefly and started to sneak up on another flower with his camera. He was wearing a blue suit with very wide lapels, the kind of lapels you might see on a giant stingray from the depths of the ocean. He also wore big black boots that made him look taller. He snapped the picture and I blinked in the light of the flash.

"Like flowers, do you, Eddie?"

"Taking pictures is clean work, Vic. That's what I like, clean work."

"Next to godliness, right?"

"Hunh?"

"How come you're taking pictures of the flowers, Eddie?"

"Charlie told me to do it. He said he needed them. He told me to take pictures of all the flowers that weren't orchids. So Antonio pointed them out and I got busy. You know, Vic, I think I'd rather be a photographer than a private detective. It's nicer somehow and you get to take pictures of plenty of girls."

"Why does Charlie want pictures of flowers?" I asked.

"He didn't say. Maybe he wants to brighten up his office."

Maybe he just wants to keep you out of trouble, I thought. But I didn't say it out loud. "Keep up the good work, Eddie, and don't put your finger over the lens."

I walked back through the rain to the shed row where the stable hand's lounge was located, although to call it a lounge was like calling an outhouse a powder room. The grass got my feet all wet and raindrops dripped off my coat onto my knees. The shed row with the lounge was the same shed row where Randall Hanks had had his office. A light was on inside. Glancing through the window, I saw Croteau and Brenda Stanley talking together. They stood with their backs to me, and I paused because I was surprised to see them together, considering the bad feelings which I had thought they had for each other. They weren't exactly laughing but neither were they sneering and shaking their fists. Not wanting to be seen peeking into the office, I hurried on but I felt heartened by the adaptability of human nature. Even if they were only trading soup recipes or discussing a sick horse or planning a bank robbery, they were at least swapping words.

The kid who I had hired to catch the rats was by himself in the lounge (maybe hangout would be a better word) with a big cage of twenty of the prettiest rats I had ever seen. They were fat, enthusiastic rats, eager to do mischief. They made powerful squeaking noises.

"I wasn't sure you'd be coming," said the kid. He wore jeans and a jean jacket and looked damp. His young face was flushed and healthy-looking.

"A promise is a promise," I said, wondering how many I had ever broken. The number "several thousand" was probably about right.

"It's just that most of the other guys have gone and I'm supposed to be leaving too."

"You get fired?" I asked.

"Mr. Croteau and Miss Stanley laid off a bunch of us, said that the farm was closing down for a while. Only about four guys are staying."

"What about the horses at Belmont?" I asked.

"That'll go on, and they're shipping about six more horses down there. A couple of guys are going with them. Lucky conversation. I squeaked and they squeaked. Soon I got pretty good at it. God knows what I was saying and I hoped I wasn't making promises I couldn't keep.

After a few minutes of rat chat, I carried the cage up to the second-floor bedroom. They were an active bunch of light-hearted creatures and they scampered over each other's backs wondering what excitement lay ahead. The cage was about two feet by two feet with a little sliding door at one end. Seeing their bright eyes and general youthful demeanor, I grieved, briefly, for their future. It's hard to be a young rat in today's hardhearted world. Rush, rush, rush—no wonder the little things get ulcers and only peck at their cheese. But with me, the rats had a chance. Out at Battlefield Farms they would have been hunted down or left to eat rat poison. Survival of the fittest, isn't that what this trifling disagreement between me and Ernie was about?

I opened the door to the empty closet. At the rear was a panel, about two feet by two feet, which led to the closet in Ernie and Puma's bedroom. I quietly unscrewed it, set it aside and peeked through the opening. Ernie and Puma kept their closet a real mess. Shoes, underwear, leather paraphernalia, spare motorcycle parts—all lay in a heap. Their closet door was open about six inches and through the opening I could see the corner of a mattress lying on the floor and at the end of that mattress was a big hairy foot with a set of the ugliest toenails I had ever seen on a living human being. I stuck my head partway through the hole hoping to catch a glimpse of Puma's lithe naked frame, but no luck. However, I could hear snoring, both a pleasant alto and a bearlike bass. I crept back out of the closet and turned my attention to my rats.

They were still dashing about with hey-hey-hey expressions. Quietly I lifted the cage, set it in the closet, raised its sliding door and waited. The rats had their freedom, and the

devils. You can have fun down there, or so I hear." The kid shuffled his feet as he talked and scratched at one of his freckles.

"How old are you?" I asked.

"Seventeen."

"And where will you go?"

"My folks live over in Greenwich. I'll go home for a bit. Least I'll have some money to help them out with, while I look for another job. The troopers wanted all our addresses so they could find us if they need to."

I wanted to tell the kid he should finish high school and stuff like that, but I figured a lot of people had already given him similar advice and I hated to be a ditto mark. I took out my wallet, pulled out four fifties and an extra twenty and handed him the money.

"Hey, thanks," he said.

"It's a pleasure to do business with you."

"Mind if I ask you a question?"

"What's that?"

"What're you going to do with all these rats?"

"I'm going to give a pal a helluva surprise."

The kid carried the cage up to the Mercedes and I walked back through the rain. As I was rounding the shed row, I nearly bumped into Brenda Stanley, who was peering into one of the stalls. She looked at me first with surprise, then suspicion, then she gave me a little smile. She was wearing a black slicker and her blond hair poked demurely from under her black rain hat.

"I didn't think you'd still be around here," she said.

"A little buying and selling took place of an innocent nature. I got myself some fat little rats."

Her smile broadened to indicate she assumed I was joking.

"So you're shutting down the farm?" I asked.

"Just for a month or so, until all this business is straightened out."

"Did Croteau tell you about Laurel Hill Farms?"

Brenda cocked her head and looked surprised. "He did, as a matter of fact. He's going to have the horses shipped back down to Belmont. I suppose I could press charges but I think it would be better if we all tried to work together."

"One big happy family."

"There's been enough divisiveness, wouldn't you agree?" She asked this a trifle aggressively.

"So the killing's over?"

"The police seem to think that Randall put the poison in that beer bottle."

"And Faber beat Hanks to death with a club. How convenient."

Brenda didn't say anything, but only stared at me from under her pretty eyelashes. She looked like she hoped it was true. I hoped so too but hope is not a commodity in which I place a lot of hope. After all, there was still the question as to who killed Bernard Logan. Had it really been McClintock? I nodded to Brenda and continued up to the parking lot, where my rats were getting wet. I stowed them in the trunk of the Mercedes and said goodbye to the kid. As I was getting ready to drive away, a state cop car pulled into the lot. The trooper behind the wheel turned out the headlights but didn't get out. I watched him crank back his seat, then I walked over. When he saw me coming, he rolled down his window and looked up at me with his loaf-of-bread face. He was an older guy, probably a few minutes short of retirement.

"You looking for someone in particular?" I asked.

He shook his head, then yawned. "Lieutenant Stachek wants someone to stay at the farm."

"So you're the official presence?"

"I guess so."

"Have a nice nap," I said.

• • •

Ernie Flako was a late sleeper. It went with the life—late nights, late mornings. I lugged the cage of rats int[o] empty duplex next to his without his shades fluttering once. It was nine-thirty on a rainy Thursday and there h[e] still collecting his Z's. Even Puma must have been s[o] asleep, and I imagined the happy couple wrapped in other's tattooed arms: a picture of connubial bliss. Afte[r] loading the rats, I drove the Mercedes over to Broadway, hurried back to the duplex under my umbrella. The Ha[ ] sat at the curb, and although I was burning to give it a l[ ] push, I forbore. When I let myself into the empty dup[ ] Ernie Flako's pit bull, named Popeye, made a few tenta[ ] growls, but they were more dutiful than suggestive of [a] real anxiety.

I had set the cage of rats in the middle of the empty roo[m] It was a nice bright space with bay windows and a firepla[ce] newly painted white walls, but I knew that as long as Er[nie] Flako and Puma remained next door, I wouldn't be able [to] rent it until racing season, and maybe not even then. It's ha[rd] being an aspiring capitalist. It means that one cannot be eg[al]itarian anymore. Like it was important to Ernie to proje[ct] the persona of a crazed serial killer from a biker movie, b[ut] did that mean he wasn't a nice guy? Of course not.

The rats stared at me expectantly. They had been makin[g] squeaking noises and darting around, but now they settle[d] down, waiting to see what came next. On an impulse I pu[t] my lower teeth against my upper lip and made a sucking noise which produced a squeak much like the one the rat[s] had been producing. Several of the rats squeaked back. adjusted my tone and soon we seemed to be having a rea[l]

only place where they could go was Ernie's bedroom. I looked at the rats and they looked back at me.

"Come on," I whispered. "Free at last, free at last."

The rats stared at me brightly. They were chipper rats but dumb rats. I made shooing motions, I shook my finger, I blew at them, I looked stern, and still the rats sat gazing at me fondly, as if, through our communal squeaking, I had become someone worthy of their respect, a kind of father figure. This went on for about five minutes and then I heard the mattress in Ernie's room begin to creak. Obviously, I didn't want Ernie to find me with the rats. Even an active imagination like mine shut down on visualizing the consequences of such a turn of events. Simply stated, he would shoot me.

Quietly, I went back to the living room. There was a stack of old *Saratogians* by the fireplace. I crumpled up several pages and lit them. When they were burning nicely, I took the bellows from the fireplace set and inhaled a bellowsful of smoke, then I hurried back upstairs.

I crouched down by the rat cage. The twenty rats were still waiting expectantly with their pert and tidy rat faces. From Ernie's room the stirrings on the mattress had resolved into a rhythmical creaking which indicated that Ernie at least was up and engaged in sexual folderol with Puma, his helpmate. He was, in the vernacular of Eddie Gillespie, putting it to her.

I stuck the nozzle of the bellows into the rat cage and fiercely squeezed the ends together, making an oooph sound and sending out a plume of smoke. Well, the rats didn't like that one tiny bit, and I might have seen disappointment on their faces had they hung around long enough for me to study them carefully. They were out of that closet in a shot.

Three seconds later Puma began to scream great big meaty

screams. This was followed by a yelp of pain from Ernie himself and then, "What the hell! What the hell!" Puma didn't stop screaming and Ernie didn't stop shouting "What the hell!" They seemed caught in a rut of violent verbal expression. Added to this clamor was the barking of Popeye the pit bull and the squealing of the rats. Truly, I was tempted to stick my head through the hole to see what was going on. But I refrained. Instead, I put the panel back in place and screwed it fast.

The yells were muted, although they continued. Suddenly, however, came a gunshot, then another. That crazy biker was shooting up my equity! He emptied the revolver, and as he was reloading I hurried downstairs to call 911. It is against the law to discharge a firearm within the city limits of Saratoga Springs without a special license. As I was talking to the officer on duty, there were more gunshots, which allowed the police department to capture the sound on tape. The noises from next door were suggestive of a Navy SEAL team at play: violence in the service of a higher purpose. I hated to think what those bullet holes would cost me.

The officer with whom I spoke swore that the police were already on their way, and, indeed, as I was walking down High Rock toward Lake Avenue, three police cars came roaring past with their lights and sirens working at fever pitch. The rain had stopped; the day was looking up. Someplace there was probably a rainbow and, if I could only locate its shining presence, it would mean good luck.

· ● ·

Around six o'clock that Thursday I was out at Charlie's place on the lake. But no longer was I a contented citizen pleased with the efficacy of police work. The day, which had begun so fortuitously, had turned into a nightmare. In fact, the entire afternoon had been spent fooling with that darn

Ernie Flako, and I had come to think that being a landlord was a punishment inflicted upon me for the sins of a past life. The whole Hindu religion began to crush me with its terrible logic.

My morning, after the adventure with the rats, had proceeded peacefully enough as I had studied the stock market and made a few wise purchases, but around noon there came a knocking on my apartment door. It was Puma. She was in tears. Ernie Flako was in jail for discharging a firearm within city limits and they couldn't make bail. He had just been hired for some maintenance job out at the track and was supposed to start on Saturday. If he was in jail, then he would lose the job. She had some crazy story about a plague of rats. She could hardly talk about it without her whole body shivering. It was a pretty body but she was wearing a bulky gray sweatshirt that covered her tattooed breasts. I don't know, maybe it was the tears. Maybe it was the memory of those tattooed breasts. Maybe it was the rats. Maybe it was a genetic flaw that sometimes allows madness to oversweep me. Whatever the case, I ended up bailing Ernie out of jail. Call me Mr. Wonderful or what?

So around three o'clock we spring him. He embraces me. He gives me a brotherhood handshake. He calls me his main man. We were standing on the sidewalk outside the police station.

"The fuckin rats, man, they were all over the place! Like it was a curse. You know, some of these houses in Saratoga are on top of Indian burial grounds. Maybe we just crossed one Indian spirit too many. How else can you explain it? The Great Beyond just decided to come and whomp us. Suddenly the whole bedroom was full of them, squeaking and running around."

"Had you been drinking?" I asked. I swear that was my only moment of subtle humor in the entire afternoon.

"No, man. I was sound asleep. Fuckin rats ran over my
back with their little feets. They got in my hair. They got in
my beard. Like they were in one fuckin hurry all over the
goddam bedroom. What could I do but haul off and shoot
them?"

"Did you hit any?"

"No, man, they were too quick and Puma was hanging
on to me screaming like a wild woman."

"What about your dog, Popeye?"

"Fuckin dog's terrified of rats, man. He put his fuckin
paws over his fuckin eyes and hid. Fuckin rats were runnin
up and down his fuckin back just like they did to us."

"How strange," I said.

"I did some damage to the walls, but I'll take care of it.
Don't you worry about a thing."

"Just don't jump bail, okay?" I asked. "Don't leave
town." I could hardly believe I was now begging him not to
do what I had earlier been praying that he would do: i.e.,
vanish.

I drove them back to the duplex which they rented from
me. I felt in some peculiar way like the victim of a shotgun
wedding. They kept expressing their gratitude to me. I
couldn't bring myself to ask about their future plans. I saw
them as remaining in my duplex, of having children and growing old in my duplex. I imagined how in the distant future
they would come to my funeral and talk about me as this
wonderful landlord who had come to their aid during a particularly scary time in their life. When I drew up behind
Ernie's Harley, I had a fierce desire to suddenly shove the
accelerator to the floor and smash into it, crush the motorcycle's shiny metal into a bumpy pancake. But I didn't. I felt
beaten. I felt there was nothing nice in my future. When they
got out, Puma kissed my cheek and Ernie gave me another

brotherhood handshake. As all this was going on, I happened to notice a rat poking its nose out from behind a bush near the front door. I nearly shied a stone at it, nasty little creature, for getting me into so much trouble.

Consequently, when I got out to Charlie's place, I felt about as cheerful as a guy who has just taken a tumble off a cliff into shark-infested waters. I didn't even have the strength to confide in him and tell him what I had done. Charlie would say it was somehow my fault and not understand it was a karmic punishment for a transgression in a past life, the actions of a stranger long dead.

"You look like you need a drink," said Charlie.

"Two," I said.

"With or without a maraschino cherry?"

"Double up on the cherries."

"Trouble with the stock market?" he asked gently.

"You don't know the half of it," I said.

We talked about the difficulties that life sometimes brings even to the virtuous and strong of heart as we sipped our Jack Daniel's Manhattans and watched the sun set over the lake. We both agreed that life could deal out a truckful of nasty pranks and what a shame it was that bad things so often happened to innocent people. Eventually we got around to the subject of Bernard Logan and the troubles at Battlefield Farms.

"You know what I learned today?" asked Charlie. "Bernard Logan had liver cancer. He had about two months to live."

"You're kidding," I said. "Did he know it?"

"Sure. It had been going on for about four months. They treated it but it kept spreading. Logan didn't want chemotherapy."

I tried to remember how Logan had looked, maybe a little

gray-faced and unhealthy. I felt sorry for the guy. "So he was just waiting? No wonder he wasn't paying any attention to the farm. I guess no one else knew about it."

"He wanted to keep it a secret."

"If it had been common knowledge, then he probably wouldn't have been murdered."

Charlie didn't say anything about that. We were sitting on a pair of rickety lawn chairs facing the water. A guy with a metal rowboat was way out in the lake trying his luck with the bass. He had a red felt hat that shone in the last light of the sun. I sipped my drink and thought about what might have happened if people had known about Logan's cancer.

"Tell me," said Charlie at last, "who were the strongest suspects and the ones with the strongest motive?"

"Randall Hanks and Brenda Stanley," I said. "That's what Logan said himself."

"But what if they were innocent, then what would Hanks and Brenda have thought?"

I considered this for a moment. "They would have thought they were being framed, most likely by the person who had actually committed the murder."

"So perhaps Hanks really did feel that he was being framed by McClintock and felt that McClintock himself was the murderer." Charlie rolled his drink back and forth in his hands. The ice made a clinking noise.

"Then Hanks might have killed him and made it look like suicide."

"But what if McClintock had nothing to do with Logan's death and what if Randall finally realized this?"

"Then I guess that Hanks would have suspected either Croteau or Faber. Maybe both."

"But what if Croteau and Faber had nothing to do with Logan's death either?"

"This is getting pretty complicated, Charlie."

"Okay, but what if?"

The fisherman with the red hat was reeling in something. I paused to watch. Maybe it was a tire, maybe a fish. "Then," I said after a moment, "Faber and Croteau would have felt they were being framed for the murder."

"So it's very possible that Hanks and Faber really did kill each other and may even have had help from Brenda Stanley and Croteau."

"Sure. I mean, I guess so."

"Well, let's say that none of those people had anything to do with Logan's death. Now Brenda and Croteau are left. What are they going to think?"

"They're still going to think they're being framed, presumably by some third party."

"And who would that be?"

I thought a moment. "Carl Logan?"

"I'm afraid so."

"You mean he killed his own father?"

"No," said Charlie, "I mean that Croteau and Brenda Stanley could suspect him of doing it and suspect him of trying to frame them for the job."

"You know," I said, "when I was out at the farm this morning, I saw Brenda and Croteau talking to each other. They weren't fighting or arguing. They were talking seriously. Is Eddie Gillespie still out there?"

"No, he finished his work around noon."

"How come he was taking pictures of flowers?"

"It's an idea I have but maybe it won't amount to anything. Who else was out there?"

"Most of the hands were being laid off. I guess Carl was around somewhere. And there was an old state trooper napping in his car."

Charlie dumped the rest of his drink out on the grass, shoved his hat on his head and got to his feet.

"What's up?" I asked.

"I think we'd better go out there."

Ten minutes later I was driving out Battlefield Road. The sun had set and the sky was dark to the east. I was driving fast because I kept thinking that I liked Carl Logan and I didn't want anything to happen to him.

"Did you bring your revolver?" I asked Charlie.

"No, I left it in town. It's in my safe."

"That's a good place for it."

"What about you? Are you armed?"

"Jesus, Charlie, you know you don't let me carry a gun."

"Pity," said Charlie.

My headlights cut across the fields and hedgerows. Lights were burning in the houses we passed. In some houses men and women were settling down to evenings of domestic bliss, in others to evenings of domestic despair. Like it's a toss-up, right?

11

It was dark when we reached the driveway leading up the hill to Battlefield Farms. A warm evening breeze blew through the windows, that spring smell of damp earth. Out there someplace the worms and bugs were all doing their jobs making the grass grow, the dirt work. I cut the lights and turned up the driveway toward the house. Both Charlie and I were uneasy, and I hoped the old state trooper was still snoozing in his car. It seemed only one light was on in the big house, maybe a lamp in the living room. I pulled around to the parking lot by the greenhouse. Although there were several cars, no cop car was among them, and the greenhouse was dark. I would have even been glad to see Eddie Gillespie's red pickup truck. Croteau's house seemed dark as well. The security lights were burning but that was it. The place looked like everybody had packed up and moved to Topeka. I parked next to Carl Logan's Toyota and turned off the engine.

"Pretty peaceful," I said.

"Like a grave," said Charlie.

We got out and shut the doors quietly. Standing in the parking lot we sniffed the air and listened. A horse whinnied. Some kind of night bird made a gloomy cry. Down the hill

I could hear a big truck on Route 4 rumbling its guts out as it headed toward Mechanicville.

"Let's see if Brenda's home," said Charlie.

We walked across the grass to the front door of the house. I don't why I felt so jumpy, maybe it was the very emptiness of the place which gave the farm a ghostliness. I don't like horror movies either; too many nasty pictures get stuck in my head. Charlie motioned me to stand back, then he went up and rang the doorbell. From inside came the muted notes of "The Yellow Rose of Texas." We waited; no one came. Again Charlie pushed the doorbell and again we listened to that silly song. Its buoyancy was more depressing than uplifting. Charlie tried the door. It was locked. He moved back to where I stood.

"Let's try Croteau's place," he said.

Since both Brenda and Carl lived in the big house, one had to assume they were somewhere else. That was one of those nifty, professional detective ideas: logical, precise, but not necessarily true. I wondered what had happened to Antonio, the gardener. Perhaps he could protect us with his bug spray. Why did I think we were in need of protection? It was one of those humid nights when the air is like wet blotting paper. East toward the Green Mountains I could see lightning. Maybe it was just the weather that was making me nervous. Again we walked across the grass in order to make no noise. It seemed if Carl Logan's Toyota was in the parking lot, then he had to be someplace on the farm.

Croteau's doorbell was a simple dingdong chime. I admired him for it. Charlie pushed it three times. I stood back about twelve feet and waited. The porch light was off but there was a light burning someplace back in the house. I wondered what had happened to the two golden retrievers. Very likely they belonged to a stable hand who had taken them away. Even most of the rats were gone. At the very moment that Charlie and I were prowling around, they were busily making themselves a new home in my duplex.

"Let's try the shed rows," said Charlie. His voice had a new urgency and I thought about how his .38 was locked up in his safe in Saratoga, where nobody could steal it, or use it.

My shoes were sopping wet from the grass and the socks were uncomfortably bunched under my clammy toes. We hurried across the yard, making a wide detour to avoid the security lights, then paused under the large oak tree. There were no lights in the bunkhouse used by the stable hands, nor were there lights on in either of the two shed rows. We investigated them in any case, moving around the outside of the buildings. The top halves of most of the doors were open and several horses had their heads stuck out into the evening air. One of them snorted at me and I jumped about a foot and grabbed Charlie's arm.

"Cut it out," he growled. "Do you always have to fool around?"

Do you see how even your friends can turn against you?

The lights were out in Randall Hanks's office. Something about his office started nagging at me, like it was something important for me to remember. There was no activity in the horse barn, although a light was burning in Frankie Faber's office. Someplace or other poor Frankie was stretched out on a slab and Randall was on another. Maybe McClintock was in the same place. I hoped at least they were side by side, swapping corpse jokes and being companionably cold together.

"Where're the guys?" I said. "They can't have let everyone go."

"Probably in town," said Charlie. "Let's try the hay barn."

We moved across the yard again. As we approached the

hay barn, I saw a crack of light through the big door, which was open about two or three feet. From inside I heard the snorting of a horse and then a voice, although I couldn't make out the words.

"Charlie," I said, suddenly remembering, "Randall Hanks had a .38 in the top drawer of his desk. Maybe it's still there."

"Let's see what's going on first," said Charlie.

We tiptoed forward. There is something about tiptoeing after the age of fifty that makes one feel silly. Approaching the opening, I could see the movement of a horse, then one or more people. Then I recognized Brenda's blond hair. Charlie was on one side of the opening and I was on the other. It was a good thing we hadn't gone looking for Hanks's revolver. We didn't have time for it. Carl Logan would have been dead.

Logan was sitting bareback on Triclops, leaning forward and being supported by Brenda. He seemed unconscious. Croteau was on a stepladder right next to the horse, which was blindfolded with a red bandanna. They were all about twenty feet away. A rope was slung over one of the beams and a noose dangled right over Logan's head. Croteau was just taking hold of the noose while holding onto Logan's shoulder. The horse kept stamping his big hooves, snorting and tossing his head, while Brenda tried to steady him. Like the horse knew there were rats nearby even if he couldn't see them. Stuck in Croteau's belt was a revolver.

"Hold the horse, dammit!" he kept saying.

"You're frightening him!" said Brenda.

Charlie started to step into the barn but I stopped him. "Wait," I said.

Croteau almost had the rope over Carl's head. I put my lower teeth against my upper lip and tried the rat squeak which had been so successful that morning. The trouble was that my mouth was dry. I was so nervous that I had used up all my spit. I worked my tongue, then tried again. A fine high squeaking noise wafted into the barn. Happy rat chat.

Well, Triclops liked that squeak about as much as a pig likes a butcher shop. He whinnied in terror and reared up. What had been a static scene suddenly became an active scene. Logan fell off Triclops's back and Croteau was knocked from his stepladder. Brenda Stanley tried to hang on to the horse's halter, but was shoved aside. Triclops kept stamping, seeking out those imaginary rats, as Croteau and Brenda scrambled out of the way. I kept squeaking. It was something I had become good at, like if Ted Mack still had his amateur hour I would have been a real contender. Triclops looked like he was trying to tap-dance. Fred Astaire couldn't have done it any better. Croteau and Brenda were busy trying to avoid those mean-looking hooves. Carl Logan had fallen off the back of the horse, then rolled away. He didn't seem in any immediate danger, at least from the horse.

All of Triclops's rearing and plunging at last dislodged the red bandanna from his eyes, allowing him to peek over the top. He caught sight of the partly open door where Charlie and I were hiding and he took off. As I say, the door was only open about two and a half feet, but that didn't bother Triclops any. He hit the opening, pushing the doors further aside, knocked me roughly out of the way and burst into the night air. I could almost feel his wonderful sense of freedom and release. Unfortunately, I had been shoved backward and fell to the ground, hard.

From inside the barn, I heard Croteau begin to shout, "Then I'll just shoot him!"

"No," yelled Brenda, "use the rope! Here, grab his arm. Put that gun away."

"Hold it!" said Charlie.

I must say that he spoke with all the authority of someone

backed up by a regiment of Marines. Brenda and Croteau must have looked at him with surprise and even trepidation. But it didn't last. After all, they had the revolver. I saw Charlie jump aside, then there were several gunshots.

Until the bullets started flying around, I was having trouble getting to my feet. My butt hurt and my legs felt old. Gunshots, however, are a wonderful motivator. I was up on my pins and scampering back toward Hanks's office before the echo of the last shot had faded. Glancing over my shoulder at Charlie, I saw him standing with his hands above his head, but that only made me run faster.

The office door was locked but the lock was flimsy. I ran at the door, smacking into it with my shoulder and hip. There came the sound of cracking wood, although maybe half of the sound derived from my bones. The door popped open. I stumbled toward the desk and pulled open the belly drawer. The .38 was just where I had last seen it. I checked again to make sure it was loaded. Then I looked around for more shells but I couldn't find the box. So I had six bullets. There was a phone on the desk and I dialed the operator.

"Get Lieutenant Stachek of the state police and tell him to get out to Battlefield Farms."

"Please hold," said the operator.

There was a long ring and then a state police operator picked up the phone and identified herself as Corporal Kimberly.

"Tell Stachek to get out to Battlefield Farms right away," I said.

"Could you please tell me what this matter concerns?" asked Corporal Kimberly in a prim sort of voice.

"Bloodshed," I said, and hung up the phone.

When I got back outside, I saw a little tableau beneath the security light stuck on the front of the hay barn. Charlie still had his hands over his head. Brenda and Croteau were standing in front of him and Croteau had a pistol. Seated on the ground was Carl Logan, apparently conscious but not lively enough to jump to his feet and belt out "America the Beautiful." I began to make my way toward the barn, keeping the oak tree between me and Croteau. What I was going to do after I reached the oak tree, I hadn't decided.

Croteau was furious but he was also uncertain. He needed to have both Charlie and Carl dead, but he wasn't sure how to go about it. Brenda was frightened but she had already invested heavily in the path of wickedness and it was a little late to buy stock in any thoroughfare. Righteousness, goodness and virtue were already beyond the range of her pocketbook.

When I got to the oak tree, I heard Croteau saying, "It will look like Carl killed him. Come on, we've got no choice!"

"Two people," said Brenda.

"You already killed Faber—how's this going to change things?"

"But she killed him out of passion," said Charlie, "because she thought he'd killed her lover. Maybe it was you who killed Mr. Hanks."

"Shut up!" said Croteau.

He swung the gun toward Charlie and possibly he would have put a bullet in him. I was still thirty feet away and afraid of shooting. Like when I shoot a gun, if I have my eyes open or my eyes shut, it seems to make no difference.

But we had forgotten about Triclops, who was still galloping around in the dark. He was one mentally disturbed animal, and suddenly he came rushing around the corner of the barn. First he wasn't there, then he was, rearing up and whinnying. Croteau's gun discharged but it must have been by accident. I saw Charlie dive back into the barn. Carl Logan lay on the ground with his hands over his head. Croteau fell backward. And then Triclops was gone again.

Croteau jumped to his feet, meaning to follow Charlie into the barn. That was the moment I took a shot at him.

I didn't hit him. I don't think I even hit the barn, but the effect was as if I had stuck a needle in his buttocks. He dropped to one knee and began whanging off shots in my direction. One hit the oak tree with a thunk and I felt sorry for it but I didn't plan on moving. It was a thick tree and a lot fatter than I was. I lay down on my belly and stuck my nose over one of the roots. Then I took another shot. The bullet banged off something metallic, which made me happy because otherwise I would have suspected that I was firing blanks.

Croteau was ducked down trying to get a bead on me. Logan was crawling away around the corner of the barn. Brenda Stanley had scampered off someplace. I must say that Croteau was a single-minded cuss. Having turned his attention to me, he seemed to have forgotten everything else.

I shouted to him, "Throw down your gun!" It seemed vital that I keep his mind on what I was doing, because Charlie was back there someplace and presumably he had his own plans.

Croteau took another shot at me, knocking a few leaves off the oak tree and terrifying the squirrels. Then I saw Charlie in the doorway of the barn. He had a long metal pole and he took a swing at Croteau. Unfortunately, Croteau caught a glimpse of him and jumped aside. The pole smacked him on the arm. Charlie then had no choice but to dive at the guy. I should say that Charlie is no fighter and he was twenty years older, but he's got a lot of heart. He's got all the heart of Joe Louis or Muhammad Ali. The two of them wrestled on the ground and Croteau got in some good hits. As I ran toward them across the grass, my belly knocked against my ribs and my knees snapped, crackled and popped like a noisy bowl of Kellogg's Rice Krispies.

Croteau slammed Charlie across the face with the side of his revolver, then turned the gun on him. That was the moment when I shoved the barrel of Hanks's .38 into Croteau's ear.

"You're a dead man if you don't drop it," I said.

He dropped it.

Charlie grabbed the revolver and scrambled out from under Croteau.

"Lie down on your stomach!" he ordered.

Croteau flopped down on his belly. He had a depressed look about him. Charlie pulled his belt free and began tying Croteau's hands behind his back. I kept glancing around for Brenda, afraid that she might show up with a tank or something.

There was a scream and then shouting from around the side of the barn. I hurried off in that direction. Maybe it was time for me to take Jane Fonda aerobic lessons and get in shape. Maybe I could be an athlete after all. With every lumbering step my body howled out its basso profundo protest: oomph, oomph.

Carl Logan and Brenda Stanley were wrestling on the ground. Logan obviously was bigger and stronger but he was also under the weather and so Brenda was holding her own.

I rapped her a couple of times on the head with the barrel of her lover's revolver. "Knock, knock," I said, "look who's here." She stopped wrestling, all the spice went right out of her. She sat on the ground rubbing her head.

"You're a pig," she said.

"But at least I'm not a murderer," I answered. "Carl, tie her hands with your belt."

A few minutes later Donald Croteau and Brenda Stanley were sitting with their backs to the barn door. Charlie stood facing them, holding Croteau's revolver. I had told them that

I had called the police and we were eagerly awaiting their arrival. Carl was talking.

"Donald telephoned, asking me to come over and talk to him. I entered his house and didn't see him. He grabbed me from behind and covered my mouth with something. It smelled like ether or chloroform. Then I passed out."

"And you would simply have been another unfortunate suicide," said Charlie.

"Stachek would have been pretty pissed," I said.

"Sure," said Charlie, "but if these two kept their mouths shut, the whole business might never even have come to trial."

Croteau was furious. It was the most emotion I'd seen the guy display. He could hardly talk without spitting.

"He killed his father! He was the one who started all this! He killed him and then tried to frame Brenda and Randall."

"That's crazy!" said Carl.

"What proof do you have of that?" I asked. I was surprised by Croteau's vehemence and I glanced at Carl, wondering if it was possible.

"Because nobody else did it," said Croteau. "Hanks and Brenda were innocent. McClintock didn't do it. Faber was down at Belmont and I sure didn't do it. We were fools. Carl arranged this whole thing."

"No," said Carl, "I loved my father." Carl seemed equally upset and hurt by the accusation.

"You're mistaken about that," Charlie told Croteau. He paused and glanced out across the yard. We could hear Triclops galloping through the dark, whinnying and stamping around. "Bernard Logan took his own life."

"That's bullshit!" said Croteau.

"Why in the world . . ." began Brenda.

I made some noises as well. Carl just watched Charlie. I got to say that Charlie loves his moments. Like he's a detective, right?

"Logan had cancer," said Charlie. "He had two or three months to live. The only person he cared about at the farm was his son, Carl. His wife was having an affair with a jerk. His stepson was cheating him by having his best horses claimed by a stable which Croteau secretly owned. And if Logan died, then what? Croteau would become the major shareholder with forty percent of the farm. Carl would have thirty-five percent and Brenda twenty-five percent. Also Brenda would be free to marry Randall Hanks. If Logan died, then his enemies would get what they wanted, while his own son would be pushed out of the way.

"So he committed suicide, although I'm not quite sure yet how he did it. But I know he ordered the rats. One hundred Norwegian rats from Jackson Lab in Bar Harbor, which he got through a friend of his in the biology department at SUNY Albany. And in Logan's bedroom are a whole bunch of novels by Dick Francis and in one of them a horse is driven crazy by electric shocks, just like Triclops.

"Logan put the cage of rats over the stall," said Charlie. "He put the cattle prod in Hanks's office and he probably even attached the horseshoe to the baseball bat. Then he drove into Saratoga and told Victor that his wife and her lover were planning to murder him. He got us to come out here and when we arrived he was dead, suspiciously dead. He knew the people he was dealing with. He hoped their guilt and fear and greed would lead them to destroy each other, and that's what they did. You two will be sent to jail for a long time."

A string of cop cars with their lights flashing made the turn around the big house toward the parking lot. In the glare of their headlights, I again saw Triclops galloping across the yard, tossing his mane and full of equine frenzy. Brenda had her head lowered but she wasn't crying, most likely she was counting her regrets. It would have been a big pile. Croteau was clenching his jaw so hard that I thought his teeth might snap. He had hated Bernard Logan more than anything and the old man had beaten him.

"So the biggest rat of all was Logan," I said. "What a guy!"

12

The Spa City Diner on South Broadway in Saratoga Springs is basically a Greek joint posing as traditional American cuisine. Pancakes, steak and eggs, plastic flowers—it has all the aspirations of home cooking, but lurking at the corners of its menu are moussaka and lamb and rice. It is Zorba the Greek dolled up in one of Betsy Ross's dresses. That's why I like the Spa City Diner. Its social pretensions resemble my social pretensions. We both pretend to be classier than we are. The restaurant is a long sprawling building with a facade of fake fieldstone and up on the roof above the front door is a plaster pony more or less full-size because this is Saratoga and horses, even plaster ones, make our hearts beat fast.

I met Charlie there for breakfast on Saturday morning. The Queen of Softness was with me and we were celebrating some good fortune, which I will get to in a moment. I was about as happy as a turtle in midsummer toasting himself on a log and I kept giving Rosemary little pats to indicate that she was never far from my thoughts. Charlie was supposed to be at the diner with Janey Burris, the registered nurse who quickens his blood and makes sure he takes his daily vitamins. As I say, I am very partial to Janey Burris but she is a little scrawny, more like a snack than a meal, if you get my meaning.

I parked the Mercedes in the parking lot and we climbed out. The restaurant also doubles as the bus station and often there are lots of people milling around, but this morning maybe one hundred people were cooling their heels outside and it looked like a mild protest about the cooking, or I don't know what, because everyone was in the parking lot and no one was inside the restaurant activating their molars. Then I heard the police cars. I took a doleful-looking guy aside and asked what the problem was.

"A bomb scare," he said, chewing the last of his pancakes. "Maybe it's the Turks, maybe the Macedonians."

Rosemary and I made our way through the crowd, looking for Charlie and Janey. The Queen of Softness was wearing a red dress of some taffeta material which swirled out around her knees so she took up a lot of space. Her milky-white bosom was all that a milky bosom should be. She wore a red hat with lots of brim and her face was prettily powdered and painted: lips like the twin halves of crimson peaches. I saw some younger men staring at Rosemary in alarm. They were neophytes dawdling in the vestibule of love who had yet to wipe their feet, enter the mansion's majestic halls and cast their bodies down upon the varieties of furniture to be found therein. I was wearing my best gray suit and we cut a swath through the breakfast-deprived crowd like a hot knife through a stick of butter. Like I say, I was happy and my smile was like an airport beacon.

Charlie's lousy little red Mazda was parked around the side and he and Janey were leaning against it. They looked cheerful enough, but compared to me and the Queen of Softness, they were like the moon competing with the sun. Charlie had a black eye from where Donald Croteau had bopped him and Janey kept consoling him about it. Charlie seemed appreciative. Like we should always have something like an artificial black eye which we can stick to our face in times of emotional need.

Janey gave Rosemary and her clothes a surprised look, then smiled. It was a nice smile, rather than a mean smile. She was wearing a blue jogging outfit and her dark hair was short and pixie-esque. Charlie saw us and his eyebrows went up. He took off his porkpie hat and made a little bow to Rosemary.

"Nice dress," he said.

"Sweet hat," said Rosemary. She kissed his cheek, leaving on his jowl a red Cupid bow souvenir of her visit.

"Hey, hey, hey," I said. "It looks like Bruegger's Bagel Bakery after all."

But it was a warm morning toward the end of May and the sun was up there doing its job with no clouds to push it around. The crowd, although foodless, was cheerful, and there was still the off chance that the Spa City Diner might be blown to smithereens, which was an event we would have hated to miss.

A waitress in a blue-and-white waitress uniform had ducked out the back with a couple of carafes of coffee and a stack of paper cups and she headed toward the four of us.

"I'm afraid it's only black," she said.

But that was fine with us and we all took a steaming cup.

"Nice dress," she told Rosemary, and I gave the Queen of Softness another pat.

We sipped our coffee and watched the Saratoga bomb squad—a depressed bunch of nervous coppers—tiptoe into the Spa City Diner hoping not to meet their eternal reward on such a pleasant spring morning. Other cops tried to shoo people away but no one paid much attention. After all, we were hungry and eager for the prospect of spectacle. The four of us talked about the weather and what a good spring it had been. Charlie had his arm around Janey Burris and she kept smiling at him as if she thought the cat's pajamas placed a distant second to his charm. Rosemary said they should come over for dinner that night and they were discussing it. But me, I could no longer tolerate the waiting and suspense and I asked Charlie:

"Charlie, just what was Eddie Gillespie doing taking those photographs in the greenhouse?"

"You mean of the flowers?" asked Charlie innocently.

"No, I mean of Antonio's legs. Sure I mean the flowers and I mean the flowers rather than the orchids."

Charlie sipped his coffee and made himself comfortable against his Mazda: a squirrelly, deficient car. His hat was pushed back on his head and his forehead was already growing pink from the sun. "I guess my question from the beginning was how did Bernard Logan die, and when I reached the conclusion of suicide, then I couldn't believe that he had just waited around for that horse to kick him to death."

"That would be quite brave," said Janey.

"Too crazy," I said. "But why the flowers?"

"There are many poisonous flowers," said Charlie in a slightly professorial tone. "For instance, almost any part of a common rhododendron will kill you within six hours and lily of the valley is even faster."

"Neither of those plants were in the greenhouse," I said.

"But he had quite a few tropical plants from all over the world. Actually there were about twenty. Eddie got Polaroid pictures of them, then took them down to a plant specialist at SUNY Albany."

"And what did he find?" asked the Queen of Softness.

"One of the plants was tanghin, a flower from Madagascar, although it's also to be found in Hawaii. Maybe you remember it, Victor, it has lovely star-shaped flowers and a very sweet smell, almost sickly."

"And?" I asked. He knows that I hate to be called "Victor" in front of Rosemary.

"Several of the seeds will kill a person in about three seconds. The effect is like a strong dose of digitalis, so that in an autopsy it could easily show up as a heart attack."

We stood thinking about that for a moment as the bomb squad continued to poke through the diner.

"So let's see if I've got this right," I said. "Logan gets a whole bunch of rats from Jackson Lab and terrifies Triclops by giving him a nasty shock every time a rat wanders by. Then Logan rigs up this cage above the stall with a string to the cage door. Next he takes a couple of these tanghin seeds, pops them in his mouth and keels over. When he keels over, he yanks the string, which dumps about one hundred rats on Triclops's head, which produces one hysterical horse. In leaping around his stall, Triclops tramps up and down on Logan's corpse, making it seem that Triclops killed him."

"Poor horse," said Rosemary. "I hope he doesn't feel responsible."

"Why did you suspect him?" Janey asked Charlie. She had her arm around his shoulder and was sipping her coffee.

"If we hadn't shown up," said Charlie, "his death might have been seen as an accident. He wanted the suggestion of murder because he wanted Croteau and Brenda Stanley and the others to start suspecting each other. So he came into Saratoga to hire a private detective. But Victor, instead of telling Logan that my usual fee was one hundred and fifty, said it was one thousand, and Logan barely blinked at that. Also, he wanted us out at the farm at a specific time—that is, at the time when he had planned his suicide. Then there was that other stuff. Logan pretended that Brenda had taken out a large insurance policy on him, but he had done it himself, then accused her of having done it. And if someone else was responsible for Logan's death, then why hadn't he or she removed the rat cage and done a better job of getting rid of the cattle prod and that baseball bat? Logan wanted them to be found, because each one threw suspicion on someone at the farm."

"He wanted to get rid of everyone at the farm except his son," I said, "but he nearly got rid of him as well."

"I don't think he necessarily wanted to get rid of Neil McClintock," said Charlie, "but he didn't really care. You know, we were his tools as much as the rat cage and cattle prod and baseball bat. I feel bad about that. We went out there and asked a lot of questions and got people anxious, with the result that Hanks killed McClintock and started the whole business."

"And Logan got away with all that," said Janey.

"Brenda and Croteau will go to jail and stay there," said Charlie. "Logan knew the people he was dealing with. He knew he could count on their being murderous in the right situation."

"And the farm?" I asked.

"Croteau and Stanley won't necessarily lose their share. Although they benefited from their crimes, they already owned their portions of the farm before they did anything wrong. However, the farm is going to be tied up in the courts for quite a while. As for Carl, I don't think he wants it. Too many bad memories. I wouldn't be surprised if he sold out and started a new farm someplace else."

"So Battlefield Farms will probably turn into a subdivision of ugly little houses," I said. "Or maybe a Revolutionary War theme park."

"It's certainly possible," said Charlie.

I didn't suppose that Bernard Logan would like that prospect, but neither did I think that he was looking down from some cloud with his harp and halo and shaking his head.

The Saratoga bomb squad came filing out of the Spa City Diner. They were looking more chipper. No bomb today. Like lifeguards, they liked their job best when nothing happened. The cops stretched, patted their bellies, then got back in their cars and drove away. People began reentering the restaurant.

"Still up for pancakes?" asked Charlie.

We were.

"By the way," Charlie asked me, "what's this fantastic news you said you had heard?"

Rosemary looked surprised, then glanced at me from under her large red hat. "Fantastic news? I thought you said it was awful news. Vic heard from his son Matthew in Chicago: his granddaughter won't be coming next month after all."

"They seem to think I'm a disreputable character," I said.

Charlie took off his porkpie hat, looked inside it, then put it back on his head. "I wonder where they got such an idea," he said. "It's positively satanic."

Sly, isn't he?